SHAKE THAT SASS

DIRE WOLF MATES
BOOK ONE

C.D. GORRI

BLURB

He's an Alpha looking for a home.
She's an outsider with no one to call her own.

Can they find what they're searching for in each other?

Derrick Rand is an Alpha Dire Wolf, a rare and powerful species of Shifter. When he hears about the seemingly ideal town of Blue Valley, New Jersey, he, and his crew, fill their tanks and mount their bikes for the long cross-country ride. Tired of the nomadic life, Derrick is determined to find a place to call home.

Lucy Corwyn leads a fairly simple lifestyle, moving from town to town and working crappy jobs to make ends meet. Feline Hybrid Shifters aren't exactly high enough on the food chain to claim territory.

After her junker breaks down, Lucy finds herself stranded and without funds. Time is of the essence for this not-so-big Cat. She needs to earn some fast cash to fix her car before some dumb Shifter tries to turn her into a chew toy.

Luckily, she spies a help wanted sign at a biker bar. Walking into Serious Moonlight to inquire about a job is a piece of cake, or so she thinks. Imagine her surprise when the sexy new owner turns out to be her mate… and that's not all.

The gorgeous male is not only a Dire Wolf, he's the Pack Alpha. Larger than life and chock full of testosterone, this monster is used to getting his way, but that doesn't mean Lucy will make it easy on the big guy.

No way. No how.

If the big bad Wolf wants to catch this little she-Cat, he's gonna have to *shake that sass.*

PROLOGUE

The air buzzed with electricity a split second before the loud roar of six—*no, make that seven*—magnificent, suped-up Harley Davidson motorcycles, speeding down the highway like so many bats out of Hell, reached Lucy's hypersensitive ears.

The symphony of engines drowned out all other traffic as Lucy sat criss cross applesauce on a patch of dusty weeds just off the shoulder of the parkway, right next to her old, not-so-reliable, Ford Aspire.

Her knowledge of mechanics was seriously lacking. But even Lucy knew the engineers who'd designed this particular vehicle had fallen short of their aspirations.

And then some.

As if to punctuate her point, the car let off another ghastly noise followed by a progression of thick, black smoke from the tailpipe.

The rust bucket was a constant drain on her limited funds, but Lucy had no choice but to keep fixing the clunker. And now she would have to look for a cheap mechanic at whatever town was located off this exit. South Jersey was chock full of small communities, safe for a week or more, but that was it.

There was no place left for a Shifter like her to hide for the long term. She was too submissive. Too small. And too damn tasty, according to the last Pack of Hyenas she'd run into.

"I sure love the taste of pussy cat in the morning. Gonna get a big ol' chunk of you, kitty freak," the Alpha fem taunted just before the attack.

Lucy was a fool thinking she could let her guard down at that shithole motel in Newark. It was not the place for a loner. But Lucy was so tired of running.

She'd managed to escape before the Hyena Shifter Alpha could bleed her too badly. It was nothing her healing abilities couldn't repair. Just a few smooth silver lines across her shoulder and stomach remained. But that incident still haunted

Lucy.

The hybrid curse. Unwanted. Unloved. Doomed to walk alone.

Lucy's mixed blood was the source of all her problems. Her hybrid heritage kept her from forming alliances. None of the Big Cat Prides wanted anything to do with her.

She'd been shunned, targeted, and tossed out of more towns than she cared to remember. Feline Shifters were such shits. Snooty fuckers, all of them. But what she wouldn't give for a Pride of her own.

Someplace where she belonged. A home. A family. But those were fairy tales for Lucy.

Shit. Shit. SHIT.

Her cell phone was dead. She had no food. No money. And it was getting late. Of course, her stomach decided to rumble right then.

Totally cliché for a chubby chick. But society's opinions on the perfect female body could go right to hell as far as she was concerned.

Lucy had curves. And yeah, she got them from eating. Food was the one source of comfort she could rely on.

Rrrrrr.

She rubbed her stomach. It had been twelve hours since she'd eaten her last granola bar. Much too long for a Shifter to go without feeding her animal.

She stood for a moment, head back, staring at the darkening sky, and watched the line of Harleys until she couldn't see them anymore. Dust clouds rose in the air behind each one of those mile-eating machines, and Lucy grinned like mad.

Lucky SOBs.

Damn, she'd love to jump on the back of one of those badass bikes, holding on to the rider and whooping in the air like a wild thing. Of course, in her fantasy, someone else had to drive.

Lucy had never ridden a motorcycle before. She would likely end up in a ditch if she tried.

Clumsy should be my middle name.

Despite being a Cat Shifter, graceful, she was not. Lucy could still see dust clouds shooting up into the air. She stood, staring at them a while longer. Her grin widened in its place.

Those little particles seemed like magic to her. Yeah, she knew they were nothing but grit, sand, and dirt. To Lucy, they were fairy dust.

Silly she-Cat.

A wistful sigh escaped her lips and she wrapped her arms around her body. Standing on the side of the road, broke but not broken, Lucy allowed herself a moment to dream.

Wouldn't it be wonderful if one of those big, sexy bikers was all for me? Some untamed, wild, beast of a man. A magician. Casting a spell with that powerful machine between his legs, carrying me off someplace safe and permanent.

She hugged herself tighter, head back as she made her wish. Lucy blinked slowly when she was done. She shook her head at her overactive imagination.

That's what she got for reading too many romance novels. Her inner beastie stirred, reminding her of her situation. She had an empty stomach, and a broken down vehicle.

Rrrrrr.

Oh well. No use sitting there dreaming stuff and nonsense when she had to keep moving to stay alive. She felt a great sense of loss when she could no longer hear the motors or see the dust clouds in the air.

What was wrong with her? They were just a bunch of strangers, for fuck's sake. Just some guys on motorcycles, passing through life without a care in the world, and that was all they were.

None of them were for her. No one ever was. Didn't Lucy have enough drama in her life?

No men.

That was her one, unbreakable, firm, completely non-negotiable rule. She was not going to fall into that trap. Not after witnessing what her mother had gone through time and again.

Pitiful, just pitiful. Don't waste wishes on men. It ain't worth it.

Those bikers rocketed down the black asphalt wherever the hell they were going on the backs of their powerful, and apparently dependable wheels, without a care in the world. Unlike her.

Shit.

Night was falling and Lucy had to get a move on. She started walking, taking the exit she should have been driving down on foot. Thank goodness her sneakers still had some sole left to them.

She turned her head, looking down the empty road. There had to be some place she could charge her cell phone and call for a tow.

The sounds of engines and horns caught her attention. Too far away to make out yet. But at least now she had a direction.

The moon was almost full, hanging bright and low in the sky. Horns meant traffic, and traffic meant people. Lucy took a long, deep breath, then exhaled. She'd wasted too much time mooning after those motorcycles.

But sometimes dreaming was all a person had. What could a little fantasizing hurt while she made her way to a phone charger and maybe a little something to eat? As her sneakers ate up the miles, she played a game with herself.

What would I do if one of those big barrel-chested men were mine? Easy. I'd wrap my arms so tight around him and just hold on for dear life. My mystery man would keep me safe.

We would share secret smiles, hand holding, and deep kisses. He'd take me for rides, driving like a wild thing, taking tight corners before stopping in some abandoned meadow.

Then he'd reach around, pull me in front of him, and claim my lips with his in a bruising kiss designed to bring me to my knees.

And that's exactly where I'd go next. On my knees, unbuckling his belt, biting my lip in excitement to see what he'd hidden behind his thick denim jeans.

He'd be thick, long, and hard just for me.

Oooh yeah. Lucy could sure get behind a dream guy like that.

Meeee—ooww!

CHAPTER 1

"Dammit."

Leave it to Lucy to step in a pothole. Ugh. She rolled her ankle too. Walking it off sucked, but it was necessary.

"I was just getting to the good part of my fantasy, too," she mumbled to herself.

Pausing a minute, she hissed and spat out a curse, checking her ankle with her fingers when the wind suddenly turned. The breeze blew right in her face, bringing with it the smell of leather and motor oil.

She closed her eyes and inhaled. Her senses tingled from something unidentifiable lingering in the scent. Before she could get more from the interesting notes hidden within the air, a big flatbed rolled by.

The damned truck leaked pollution and Lucy nearly doubled over, choking. Damn sensitive feline nose of hers.

Achooo.

She growled aloud and hobbled up the driveway of the small gas station convenience store.

"Hello."

"Hi there, Miss."

Lucy's ankle throbbed. She was tired, hungry, and annoyed.

"Do you have an outlet so I can charge my phone?"

The older man nodded at where an outlet sat unused behind a shelf full of mostly expired snack cakes. Plugging in her ancient flip phone, she leaned against the wall and waited for it to charge enough to call a tow service.

The cashier was an older man, a *normal* if her nose could be trusted. He looked her over through narrowed brows, pausing when the sound of her rumbling stomach reached him.

"You can help yourself to one of those packages there. They might be a little stale, but I imagine it's better than nothing," he said, pointing to the snack cakes.

"Sorry, I'm on a budget," she muttered, embarrassment heating her cheeks.

"The company comes and swaps them out every week. They are due tomorrow morning. No one will go looking for one," he added kindly, nodding at her to go ahead.

"Okay. Thank you," she replied softly, grabbing a chocolate frosted cupcake and scarfing it down in two bites.

"Hell. Have two then, child. Must be starving. Go on now."

"I appreciate it," she said, looking in her pockets for loose change.

"Don't you worry about it. Look, my name is John, and I'm a widower, but my Nancy would have hated me leaving a young girl to go hungry in my store."

"That's really kind of you, John. I'm Lucy," Lucy replied, tears welling in her eyes.

"What's the matter, little lady, you okay?"

"Yeah," she mumbled, wiping her face hastily. "I'm sorry. It's been a long time since someone was kind to me."

"Look, don't you worry about the snack cakes. You can get me back some other day. You havin' car trouble or somethin'?" John's eyes were round with sympathy. He was a good soul, showing kindness to a stranger.

"Car trouble. Waiting on my phone to charge so I can call a tow," she told John, deciding to trust the honesty she heard in his voice.

"Well, I can help with that. This is a local place. You might have to haggle a bit, but he's the closest you'll find without having to pay an exorbitant amount for them to bring your car in," he told her, handing her a card.

"Thank you so much. My phone is at fifteen percent already. Do you think I can charge it a little bit more while I wait on the truck?"

"Of course, Lucy."

"Thanks, John." She offered a real smile that time, and the old man gave her a semi-toothless grin.

"Glad to help."

Lucy dialed the local mechanic's roadside assistance number while John went back to whatever he was doing behind the counter. The receptionist told her a driver was on the way, and that was that.

"All sorted?" John asked.

"Yes. Thank you so much."

"You're welcome. Good luck to you," he said, waving goodbye.

The snack cakes stopped the bite of hunger, but she would need more than that. Still, the hike back to her car was manageable at least. There was nothing else she could do about it now, anyway.

Lightning cracked overhead, splitting the sky apart and flashing brightly overhead. Thunder rolled in like an angry Mama Bear scolding her errant cubs, and Lucy shook her head as she quickened her pace.

Lucy knew all about Mama Bears. One had taken her in when she was thirteen and on the run from the fresh hell foster care had placed her. She'd had four cubs of her own, but needed the help.

At the time, Lucy had been willing to do anything for a place to sleep and a warm bed. Taking care of the cubs was easy while Jaylinn worked as a waitress at a greasy spoon down the road from the motel where she lived.

It was the kind of place that took cash every week for rent. But it had been the closest thing to home Lucy had for a long while. She liked it there.

It was the happiest time of Lucy's young life up to that point. It only lasted eight months before authorities caught up with her. Her mother's ex had called in the police, claiming he missed his stepdaughter.

Lying sack of garbage that man. He said her

mother was beside herself with worry when the foster family had misplaced her.

"Misplaced," she mumbled.

Like she was a sock or glove. Truth was, that asshole just wanted to use Lucy to keep her mother in line. It worked for a while. The sleaze had griped the entire ride back to their dirty, cramped apartment about stupid human authorities.

He'd said they had no idea what they were doing, placing a Shifter cub with normals. It bothered her that he was right about that. Keeping the secret of the supernatural world was tantamount to their survival as a species.

At thirteen she'd been on the cusp of her first change. While Jaylinn might have been able to help her through it, the Mama Bear had no time for Lucy.

She needed another Big Cat, someone more dominant to keep her steady. Preferably her mother. While that did not happen, Lucy did the best she could with her inner animal. Her hybrid Shifted form was a shocker.

"The shit really hit the fan then," she mumbled to herself.

She had a while yet for the truck to arrive, and she saw her car in the near distance where she'd left it–or rather, where it had left her.

She'd been lost in her memories as she walked. They'd rolled across her brain, like a runaway train without stops or any real destination.

An unfortunate side effect of being alone so much was talking to herself. Lucy did that a lot. She'd had time to get used to her animal, but the truth was off putting to a lot of Shifters.

Lucy was an unfortunate and somewhat curious looking combination of her mother, a sleek and petite Bobcat Shifter, and her sperm donor, a big old Mountain Lion Shifter.

She mostly resembled the latter, but smaller by a third of the average Mountain Lion Shifter. She also had the short, cropped tail, and pointed ears of her mother's beastie.

Freaky, as her stepfather had put it after that first change.

"Perfect timing," Lucy muttered as a light spattering of rain started falling.

Minutes ticked by as she hustled to her car, by then more thunder and lightning cracked across the sky, and drops fell in earnest. She fumbled with the rusted door handle.

Locked. Fuck.

Lucy checked her pockets, cursing under her breath. There was a gaping hole in the back right one. It was her favorite and most often used pocket.

Empty. Of course, it was.

"Shit," she growled.

Slamming her hands against the glass to see inside, she bent over and peeked. There they were, sitting on the driver's side like they were innocent in all this.

Stupid keys. Stupid hole in my back pocket. Stupid stupid rain.

Well, at least the tow truck was coming. John had assured her Blue Valley was only six miles or so in size. Small and close knit, that's what he'd said.

"On his way, my ass," Lucy growled and huddled into her soaked hoodie.

Two-hours had passed before the tow truck arrived. The ornery driver cursed the whole time he had to work in the rain. Took him thirty minutes to load her tiny car, and he made her stand outside the whole time.

Finally, inside, Lucy shivered uncontrollably. She was dripping in the seat next to Tony, the chubby, sweaty, and somewhat creepy tow truck driver.

She'd taken off her soaked hoodie, desperate to quell the chill racking her bones, but regretted it now. The white t-shirt she'd had on underneath clung to her skin, giving the greasy jack-off a perfect view of her abundantly large breasts.

Thanks for the tatas, Mom.

The woman hadn't given her anything else by way of genetics, but Lucy usually liked her boobs.

Not right now. But usually.

"Hey, eyes on the road," she growled and snapped her fingers at Tony the Perv.

"Oooh, spunky. I like that in a chick," he said with a leer.

She clenched her teeth against the snarl that rose in her throat. Slashing him across his stupid face would not win her any favors. So, with a great deal of strength she did not know she had in reserve, Lucy ignored the revolting man.

He was definitely icky, but he was a human, a *normal* as Shifters called them. Nothing she couldn't handle. She might be short for a female, but she was still a Shifter, which meant if Tony here got handsy, Lucy would be kicking his ass ten ways to Saturday.

Of course, if he'd been a Shifter, she would not have been so confident. A she-Cat-Mountain Lion hybrid was a bit on the low, *squishable* side of the predatory hierarchy.

Always a quick study, she'd learned early that in order to survive, Lucy had to stay out of towns and cities where the more dominant species tended to congregate.

Without a Pack, Clan, or group of her own, she was at the mercy of whatever bigger, stronger predators ruled the areas she passed through. It was a lonely existence, but it was her life. And she did just fine on her own.

Independence was crucial to Lucy. She'd watched her mom flit from male to male, seeking protection and affection time and again from anyone who would give it to her all through her troubled life.

Her mother had always been kind of desperate and sad, and nothing ever seemed to work out for her. Especially not the last time.

Lucy shuddered. She refused to be like her mother. She could and would protect herself.

What did she need a man for? Not a single thing, that's what.

As far as she was concerned, Lucy did alright. Yes, she missed her mama, even after ten years. But she was still here. No strings or ties. No anchors to slow her down. Nothing to hold her back.

Lucy might never get very far, but wherever she wound up, she would get there on her own.

She watched Tony the Perv turn the AC on,

fucker was trying to make her nipples harder beneath the chilled, soaked shirt.

Screw him. She pointed the vent away from her and grabbed her wet hoodie and backpack, clutching both to the front of her body.

"How long?"

"About fifteen minutes," he grumbled.

Curiosity about the place she was currently stranded in had Lucy turning towards the window. It was dark, and she couldn't really see much because of the rain.

But anything that kept her mind off the rank smelling cab of the tow truck, and Tony the Perv, who was currently chewing gum with his mouth open like some dull-witted cow, was alright with Lucy.

It was all she could do not to scratch his face off.

Grrrrr.

"Shit." Lucy knew she'd entered the Garden State a few miles back, but she had hoped she'd landed on the Delaware side of 95.

As they sped past the *Welcome to New Jersey* sign, those hopes were thwarted.

"Blue Valley coming up," Tony grunted.

He was right. The next sign said Blue Valley.

More followed, telling how far they were from Barvale, Maverick Point, and Maccon City.

Unfortunately, none of those towns were far enough for her liking. This part of New Jersey was run by Shifters, Big, dominant, fur-ocious Shifters. Bears, Tigers, Wolves, and even Dragons, if the rumors were true.

Oh, I am so fucked.

Everywhere she looked, there were predators. She only hoped Tony the Perv's boss was good at fixing cars. She was barely healed from her recent Hyena attack.

"What's that?"

"Nothing," she replied with a tight smile. "Um, Tony? Would you happen to know of any place I can rent a room? Somewhere quiet, on the outskirts of town, maybe?"

"Sure, I do," grinned Tony.

Lucy felt her stomach drop.

Yep, this was definitely gonna suck.

CHAPTER 2

"It's been two months, Derrick. Opening night is two days away, and we don't have enough bartenders. I'm telling you this is gonna be a disaster," Sheila shrieked and stomped her foot like a giant diaper baby brat.

His little cousin was always quick with her temper, but it was nothing Derrick could not handle. He raised an eyebrow, and clever little Wolf changed tactics, pouting, and giving him those big goo-goo eyes like she used to when she wanted him to carry her around piggyback when they were kids.

Fucking hell.

Classic Sheila. Always resorting to what he thought of as overly dramatic tactics whenever she was attempting to wrestle Derrick's attention from whatever he was doing, so he could do what she wanted instead. But not this time.

Derrick was busy AF. Okay, fine. Maybe not busy. But he was trying to settle his inner animal, and that was a hell of a thing for a dominant Dire Wolf. He'd tried everything. Doing the books, stocking the upstairs coolers, checking the kegs, and counting the number of fucking beer glasses he'd ordered for the bar.

Right now, he was outdoors in the giant barn they'd converted into a garage, polishing the body of his custom *Harley Davidson VRSCDX Night Rod Special.* Just because his small Pack of Dire Wolves had given up life on the road, didn't mean they could let things go to shit.

Hell, he still loved riding, but it had been years since his boots had stood in one place long enough to leave a print. Things were changing. The animal inside him was restless, looking for permanence. It was time to settle down.

Six months ago, he'd contacted the Shifter Council with his intentions and sent out feelers for a stable territory, nothing too big, and without any other Shifter presence, so he and his Pack could build a home. Within a few weeks, Derrick was looking at available real estate in Blue Valley, New

Jersey. The small east coast town seemed the perfect fit for him and his Pack.

That did not mean Derrick was going to abandon his wheels. A biker at heart, his love of crotch rockets had always been a huge part of him. It was what had him outside right now, cleaning, polishing, and making sure every single bit of his chopper was in top form.

Sheila should know better than to interrupt him when he was taking care of his baby. Was he wrong for being outside when they were about to launch their new business?

Maybe.

But his baby cousin knew exactly what was up when Derrick was busy with his bike, especially considering she felt the same about her own snazzy little Softail Convertible. All his Pack mates shared that same deep love and respect for their mounts. They were also all meticulous when it came to caring for them.

They were a Pack of seven strong, a blip compared to the Macconwood Wolf Pack which held most of North America under Rafe Maccon. That Alpha was good, strong, and he'd recently turned down the role of High Alpha, a position of great power over all standard Wolf Shifters. Derrick had followed their trials and tribulations under the Curse of Natalis, and its demise at the hands of a teenager from New Jersey. That young woman had accepted the role Rafe had refused and was now facing hell trying to organize and control the Werewolves of the world and their newfound powers.

All very interesting, but nothing to do with Derrick and his Pack. They were not standard Wolves. They were something else. Something rare and powerful. Seven was all he needed. Derrick's leather cut, complete with its DWMC patch, flapped in the breeze as he straightened his spine and turned to face the little redheaded menace. He sniffed the air and rolled his head on his neck. Rain was coming.

Patience, he told his beast when his cousin met his stare for a beat too long. She averted her gaze, baring her throat slightly in deference to his inherent dominance.

"Sheila, what is it you're telling me that you think I don't know?"

"We need another bartender, Derrick, or we are gonna bomb on opening night."

"And has no one answered the advertisements you sent?" he asked.

Sheila flipped her red hair and closed and opened

her mouth a few times. Sometimes, all it took to stun her into quiet was being reasonable. Fiery little brat.

"I'm just concerned," she muttered, and he could not blame her in the least.

The Pack had pooled its resources to invest in this venture, and it was a huge risk. Not only because of the money, but because they had never tried anything like this before. Dire Wolves were nomadic creatures, if not by nature, then because of circumstance.

His Pack consisted of the toughest, most loyal badasses in the world as far as Derrick was concerned. He would do everything in his power not to let them down. Especially not baby cousin over here.

"It will work out, Sheila."

"Yeah, well, I wish I had your confidence," she replied, biting her lip the same way she had when she was a nervous little kid.

"If you did, you'd be Alpha," he teased, earning him a smile.

He could hardly believe they were now the proud owners of a real life roadhouse, hovering right on the city limits of Blue Valley, New Jersey. Locals had warned him about the place. Said it got too little traffic to make ends meet, but Derrick was not worried. He had something the previous owners did not.

He was a Shifter, and as such, the supernatural community, though secret from the human world, would come check them out in droves. He hoped to woo them into a steady clientele with his unique food and beverage offerings. The bar itself was a piece of work. It had been abandoned, left to rot, but with a little elbow grease, he and the Pack got it in tiptop shape.

Everything was all neat and polished, ready for business. There were the last minute things that needed fixing, of course, and he would see to it. After he tended to his bike. Customized to fit his bulk and handle his strength by their very own mechanical expert, Cole Mingan, the big beast of a Harley, seemed to call out to the big bad Wolf inside Derrick, begging for a ride.

Cole was good at his job. So good, in fact, that Derrick had decided to give the younger Shifter charge of the twenty classic bikes he'd recently bought and had shipped here to their new permanent address. The idea was to fix them up and put them on display. Sort of a draw for motorcycle fans and would be customers.

Currently, the best looking hogs were lined up

on the far side of the roadhouse, which they'd named *Serious Moonlight* after a unanimous vote. The rest of the bikes were inside the garage, waiting to be fixed.

"Sheila," Derrick asked after a minute. "Did you advertise for bartenders and waitstaff in both the town weekly circular and the daily newspaper like I told you to?"

Sheila growled, then heaved an exasperated sigh. She was no dummy, but it didn't hurt to check.

"Course I did, cousin. But we're strangers here, and small towns on the east coast are not as friendly as I thought they would be," she replied heavily.

Sheila's growling grew louder, and when he turned, he saw her staring at the open garage doors, towards the open road. It was a problem he'd been anticipating, the call to roam. But they'd all agreed before coming here, they were committed to trying to grow roots.

Derrick stared at his cousin. Poor thing was trembling from head to toe. Her green eyes were glowing with the force of her Wolf, and fur had already started to sprout along her arms. Another reason they needed a place to settle.

"Be still," he said, using the force of his power to soothe her angsty beastie.

"Alpha?" He heard her frightened plea and understood it.

Derrick's eyes narrowed. Sheila was scared, and her pupils were dilated. He growled deep. The rough sound forcing her eyes downward. That was good. She was not too far gone yet. He used his Alpha voice, never to cow, but only to calm her emotionally heightened animal.

"This is a good place for us. I feel it, Sheila. I wouldn't steer the Pack wrong."

Sheila closed her eyes, nodding her head. She trusted him, and that was a balm to his heart. After standing perfectly still for one long, drawn out breath, she opened her eyes, and he was pleased to see her Wolf had abated.

"Everything alright?" Brock, his Beta, poked his head inside the garage. Derrick met his eyes, then waved the male away. Things were fine now.

Sheila's beast had quieted, and Derrick's felt steady after her helping her through it. That was one of the things he had not expected of being Alpha. Helping his Pack mates calmed his beast, as if he knew his place and reveled in his position.

It was not always easy, and sometimes, he downright hated it. But Derrick was born to lead, like his mama always said. It was a hard road, but he'd been born to it. Leaving life on the road for a place here was difficult for all of them, Sheila more than the rest. He understood her predicament all too well.

As the only female in the Pack, she felt more alone than the rest of them. Their mothers were off, living life in a Pack MC made up of only females. She'd gotten her invite last year but turned them down. Sheila was not ready to give up on the good things yet, and he did not blame her.

Staying put was going to be hard on all of them. Life on the road was not easy, but it was something they knew and understood. This was different. Unchartered territory. Scary and exciting.

Derrick and his Pack had eaten up mile after mile on the backs of their bikes together. They would learn to settle together as well. Pack was family. There was nothing more important than that. But even families had hierarchies, and for Dire Wolf Shifters such as they were, that meant the person who was not only the strongest, but who had the most control was the Alpha, and he was responsible for everyone.

As Alpha, it was Derrick's job to protect his Pack. Even from themselves. Helping them control their giant, prehistoric animals was one of his responsibilities. Many thought an Alpha ruled by simply dominating around those under his care. They couldn't be more wrong. Dominance and subjugation had their place, but it was Derrick's unique ability to control his urges and instincts that made him the undisputed Alpha of their Pack.

"Sorry, cousin. Thank you for helping me, uh, I think I'll call the paper again."

Sheila spoke with her eyes downcast, and her throat exposed. Derrick pulled her into a quick hug, patting her shoulder when she stepped away. Dire Wolf Shifters needed touch to settle their animals, and as Alpha he understood and craved that connection as well. He dismissed her gently, worrying his lower lip as she walked away.

"You do that, cousin. I'll be along shortly," he murmured, knowing full well she heard him.

Dire Wolf hearing was aces, even after years of listening to motorcycle engines. With that, his attention back on his bike once more.

Always take care of your Pack first, then your wheels, his late father's voice echoed in his brain as he put away the degreaser and wax.

He grabbed the few rags he'd been using and tossed them on top of his bundle, stooping to pick it up before returning it to the far side of the garage. The rain had started in earnest now, and he wondered if it would be a flash storm or something wilder and more untamed.

Their new property sat alongside an expanse of woods, and Derrick looked forward to running through the mud and tearing through the trees later on tonight in Wolf form. It was one of the perks of this spot. Edge of town, no close neighbors. There was a shopping center fifteen minutes away, but that was back on the highway. A gas station was another ten down the other way, and the road into town was a good twenty minute drive.

They were close enough to have a steady business, and far enough to not get caught in their fur. It was the main reason he'd felt drawn to the old, abandoned bar. The property came with a couple of acres of forest, as well as two other buildings and a large parking lot.

The huge, barnlike structure had already been converted into a makeshift garage. They'd just made it better. It sat at the opposite end of the bar, through the long, paved parking lot. It was perfect for storing, maintaining, and fixing up motorcycles, and the boys had all gone apeshit for it.

A few hundred yards west of the garage, past an old, wooden privacy fence he intended to have replaced with something sturdier, was an enormous two-story house. The driveway for the house was private, and far enough away from the bar to be comfortable. There was a gate in the fence and a lock, only he and his Pack had the key too. The bar crowd could not access it from the parking lot, and that was enough security for him and Sheila and the guys.

It really was some house. At first, grossly over-grown with weeds, field mice, bird's nest, and a host of cobwebs, but after some TLC it was all sparkly and fine to move in. The twelve-bedroom monster had been abandoned for some time, but someone had loved it at some point.

Derrick could see that in the stained glass windows on the doors, and the hand-painted flowers someone had put in every bedroom. The guys moaned and groaned about it, but no one had painted over them just yet. It was a little worse for wear, in truth, *all* three buildings were, but none had anything wrong with them a little spit and polish couldn't fix.

They'd been working on it for just a couple of weeks and already the place was unrecognizable. The property positively gleamed. There were new locks on the doors and windows they'd installed. Security systems in place. Cable and Wi-Fi already hooked up. Hell, there was nothing they hadn't thought of, and when they couldn't get a crew in well, Derrick and the guys, Sheila too, just dug in themselves. They'd power-washed, scrubbed, scraped, and repainted just about everything, except that flower trim inside the house.

They'd repaired or swapped out most of the outside moldings and trappings, got new TVs, and furniture galore. Sheila, Weylin, and Phoenix were into antiques and had insisted on hitting flea markets and secondhand stores as opposed to ordering everything new, which is what Derrick would have done. Still, he allowed it. It made them happy, and he could see why they preferred older digs. They simply did not make stuff the way they used to, and Dire Wolves required sturdy seats and what not.

Sheila had a real knack for things like that. The older furniture added character and comfort in the house. Lucky for them, the bar had been mostly intact on the inside. They'd had to do a massive cleanup, and the kitchen needed new appliances, but the old wood bars were good.

Thor had sanded and refinished both the front and back bars with Derrick's help until they gleamed and sparkled. Same for the floors and fixtures.

They'd ordered glasses, booze, and a few of the newer, more energy compliant fridges and coolers along with the ovens and prep tables for the kitchen.

Serious Moonlight was a bar first, but they would start with the staples. Wings, Burgers, fries, pretzels, and such. Eventually, they would bring in a larger menu for dining in. His Beta, Brock Laurent, was a talented chef, and Derrick had left him in charge of outfitting the kitchen.

This was a risk. A Huge one for a group of nomadic Shifters, but something about Blue Valley called to Derrick. It pulled him in like a magnetic pole. He sighed as he dropped the bucket of cleaning supplies. They were going to open in just a few days and everything was near perfect. Except for a few minor details. Like hiring another bartender. But all in all, Derrick was confident the Pack would make back their investment and then some.

We damn well better.

The Pack had some money, but this endeavor had taken a huge chunk of that. As Alpha, Derrick was responsible for the money, the investment, and the decision to settle in Blue Valley. Was it the right move? He sure as fuck hoped so.

His Pack was not like others. They needed this. Unique and rare even in the paranormal world, they'd traveled long and hard for an opportunity to settle in a place unoccupied by other Shifter groups. Most Shifters didn't want the trouble they brought with them.

Not that it was their fault. Not really, anyway. But that's what happened in supernatural circles, and for the sake of keeping their big secret, it was best their kind stay away from settled areas.

The issue was dominance. Dire Wolves were bigger, stronger, lived longer, and grew more powerful than most other species of Shifter. Derrick was the biggest and baddest of them all. In the past, challenges had come at him from every direction whenever he'd settled in one place for too long. It was his natural dominance combined with the fact he was a rare, and almost extinct species of Shifter.

True, their numbers were few, but they were still kicking and fuck anyone who tried to make it otherwise. Their prehistoric species of beast had died out in the wild thousands of years ago, but their Shifter relatives were still around, though rare and small in number.

The most basic difference between a Wolf Shifter and a Dire Wolf Shifter was size. In their fur, they were more than double the size of the modern Wolf Shifter. That, coupled with their unique ability to tap into elemental magic, made them special as well. His kind practically oozed power and strength.

A fact other Shifters, especially Alphas, had a hard time dealing with. He had no wish to take over other Packs, Prides, or Clans—but did they believe that?

Hell no.

Fuckers always wanted to try to take a piece of him. Not that they got close. Derrick was one hell of a fighter. His body was a testament to that. At almost seven-feet tall and two-hundred-ninety pounds of pure, rock hard muscle, he was, in a word—*efucking-normous.*

They all were.

Sheila said it was time they got lucky when he'd been sent the listing from the Shifter Council. Derrick didn't know a thing about luck, but he was damn grateful for this shot. His entire Pack—Brock, Cole, Phoenix, Weylin, Thor, and Sheila—were all grateful. So tired of life on the road, they'd broken off from their nomadic parent MC two decades ago and had almost immediately started searching for a place they could land.

The graybeards and old ladies didn't believe any town where Shifters resided, which was every town these days, would ever accept Dire Wolves in their territory. Not without a war, anyway.

It went without saying that Derrick did not want that. War was not good for anyone. He just wanted a small piece of earth to call home for him and his Pack. A place of their own where they could settle down, find mates, maybe even have cubs.

Cubs.

His Dire Wolf growled inside of him. The great black beast's loneliness was a heavy and constant presence in his heart. It was time to change that. Time to find a mate before he succumbed to the wild side of his existence—a condition that often led to death.

Once a Dire Wolf went feral, there were few who could take him out. It was often left to his Pack to do the dirty work. He did not want that for them.

Derrick watched the rain smack against the newly paved lot and breathed deep. It was true, he'd tried this before. Tried settling once or twice, but it had never felt right. He was taking a hell of a chance, but he had to for the sake of survival.

I'm not ready to call it quits. Not yet. This time will be different.

This time. This place. Derrick would make it work.

Mistakes, accidents, a misalignment of fate or whatever other reasons past attempts had failed were not an option now. Past hurts, jealousy, and bitter disappointments abounded in his memory, forever ingrained in his mind. Yes, he made damn sure he remembered them. All of them. Without memory, history repeated itself, and fuck that. Derrick refused to be a sad statistic.

The tattoos covering his massive frame told his story. The story of his Pack. Good times and bad. Every significant event in his life and the lives of his ancestors covered his arms, chest, stomach, and even his legs.

His back, though, that was bare. An empty canvas of skin and muscle. That place was reserved for his future mate, his family. He'd left it alone solely for the bonding ritual that would one day complete his mating to his one and only true mate.

He'd only ever seen it done once, and Derrick had wanted it for himself ever since that day. He wanted someone of his own. Someone to love, to protect, and cherish for all his days.

Gods willing.

CHAPTER 3

"Fucking hell."

Lucy bit her tongue as she hopped out of the smelly cab of the tow truck. The rain had finally stopped, but her hair was still wet in its messy bun, and her clothes were damp and clinging to her overheated skin.

Her she-Cat was itching to be set free, but Lucy had to get this settled first. Tony the Perv had finally gotten around to dropping her off at the old boarding house he'd mentioned, but only after his boss had quoted her an estimate for her car. Sixteen-hundred bucks to fix that pile of junk.

Mother humping butt licking poop chomping fart flakes. Rrrrrr.

It was highway robbery, dammit, but what was a

girl to do? Lucy was no mechanic. She'd only bought the old car because it was all she could find after she'd scoured the used car lot for something affordable.

The faded yellow paint with big daisy stickers all over the bumper, as well as, covering the seats of faded beige interior, had sweetened the deal. She was a sucker for aesthetics. Daisy stickers were fun, and she'd needed fun at the time. It was cute in a retro sort of way.

Of course, she'd had no idea the darn thing was going to be impossible to fix without spending a fortune. The grizzly old mechanic over at *Big Tom's Tow and Go* had given her a song about it, taking three weeks to get the special parts he had to order before it would be ready. Then it would be a waiting game of how long to take apart the engine and put it back together again.

There was no upside, as far as she could tell. But at least she was out of that tow truck. The cab had smelled like a week old tuna sub complete with onions, vinegar, and gods knew what else had been shoved under one of the seats and left to rot.

Gross, she thought to herself as she lifted her bag onto her shoulder. Ripped jeans and wet shirt clinging to her curves, Lucy grunted miserably. She should have changed into something dry after at *Big Tom's.* But with her luck, those guys would have recorded her in the bathroom.

It was a sad day for humanity when that was the first thought a girl on her own had when stranded in a strange town. But she couldn't afford to go apeshit on a couple of normals. The Shifter Council would have her ass. Screw that. Lucy could deal with wearing a wet shirt for a little while longer.

Sigh.

With all the rain, she would've thought the humidity would've lightened up, but nope. It was still humid despite the growing chill in the night air. Her shoulder length hair was piled on top of her head in a messy bun and her sneaker-clad feet squeaked a little once she hit the newly paved parking lot.

Nice. No puddles, she thought absently.

But where the hell was she? She turned in a full circle and took in the bright pink neon sign with the words *Serious Moonlight Roadhouse & Bar.* Underneath was a plastic banner that someone had tied to the pole with the words *opening soon* in bold red block letters.

Didn't look like any boarding house she'd ever

stayed in, but what did she know? There was a huge house in the next lot over. Maybe that was it.

"You lookin' for somebody?" A deep voice asked, and Lucy whipped around to see a giant stranger approach from a crouched position behind the pole that held the bright pink sign.

"Fuck a duck, you scared me!"

"Uh, sorry?"

The stranger grunted, rubbing the back of his head, but his apology sounded more like a question to Lucy. It seemed comical that such a masculine person was standing there bathed in pink light, but there it was.

She guessed he'd been working on the electrical box, and her assumptions were confirmed when he bent down and shut and locked the metal door. He had short black hair, wide shoulders, and looked big as fuck. He was wiping his hands on a rag, trying to seem less intimidating she gathered, and appreciated the effort.

"Uh, yeah, I guess, I am looking for s-someone," she replied, stuttering when a sharp breeze dragged his scent to her.

Uh oh.

The man was big, imposing, handsome in his own way, but what really concerned Lucy was the fact he smelled like Wolf. Only, the scent was different from Wolf Shifters she'd encountered before. There was something powerful, wild, and maybe a little untamed about him. Of course, that could have been his biker vest or his deep-set eyes that caused chills to run down her spine.

Shit.

"My name is Cole. Cole Mingan. You here about the job, lady?" he asked and immediately Lucy nodded.

She might not have been looking there for a job, but she did need one. From what she knew about Wolf Shifters in this part of the country, they all answered to Rafe Maccon and that Alpha was a no-nonsense kind of guy. Surely, this guy had enough sense not to attack a lone feline. Hell, he wasn't even growling, and that was all the encouragement she needed.

Desperate times, she thought, recalling the sixteen hundred dollars she needed to accrue to fix her wheels.

"Right," he growled. "Come on, this way." Cole turned to walk through the empty lot to the front door of the roadhouse.

Lucy followed, mind wandering as a result of her mild panic at following a strange predatory Shifter into a dark bar. It was almost midnight, but Shifters tended to be night owls. She wondered if it was politically incorrect to call someone a night owl if they weren't actually owls? Like, did Owl Shifters get pissed when they heard that remark?

"You alright?" Cole asked, his head cocked to the side as he waited for her to catch up.

Lucy straightened her shoulders. In her experience, it was best not to let her fear show, and she really did need a way to make some money. If they were hiring, she should at least try to get the job.

"Yep," she replied and tried to smile, but it came out more of a grimace and Cole frowned at her.

His eyes strayed to her wild hair and wet clothes, and she remembered why she was there in the first place. Lucy needed room and board. She was dead on her feet, but she also needed a job. With any luck, she'd find both right here. But probably not if Cole here thought she was a total wack job for thinking about owls and political correctness in the Shifter world.

Best keep that bit to myself.

Her thoughts could get random sometimes, but that was simply her overactive imagination at work. She followed the giant to the door he held open and walked through it with her shoulders straight and head high.

While the exterior seemed plain and simple, the interior of the place was impeccably clean and edgy. She approved the industrial look, with the ceiling exposed and open barn doors separating sections. Wood gleamed and metal shone, and Lucy could smell the myriad of cleansers they'd used along with fresh paint, stain, polyurethane, and polish to spruce the place up.

Clearly, the guys who'd bought the place had gone through a lot of trouble fixing it up. Cole did not bother showing her around. He simply stomped down the corridor and expected her to follow. Her first whiff of him already told her why.

Dog—*no matter how big or small*—always thought they were better than cats. Of course, this amused Lucy. Silly canines. Everyone knew cats were better.

Meow.

Lucy followed him down the hallway to a closed door that had the word *office* painted in thick black letters. The scent of Wolf was stronger, and dominance heavier the closer she got. Whoever was behind that door was undoubtedly the leader of this small group.

"Hey yo, Derrick! Someone's here about the job,"

Cole yelled, then turned the knob at the grunted *"send him in"* that came from inside.

"Go on," Cole said and walked away, leaving Lucy to face whoever was behind the large door.

A little nervous, and a lot desperate, she squared her shoulders and inhaled one deep breath. She wanted to get a better read on the room's inhabitant. Wolf, yes, but what kind? There were different subspecies of Shifter she'd studied in her quest to keep herself safe from big predators.

Gray Wolves. Red Wolves. Arctic Wolves. Each one with its own quirks and temperament. Maybe they were not Wolves at all. There were also other canids like Coyotes, Foxes, and Jackals to consider as well.

Shit. She was psyching herself out now. Lucy was almost panicking. The place was just too full of cleaners and fresh paint for her to get anything more than something from the *Canidae* family. More than likely, she was dealing with a bunch of Gray Wolf Shifters. They were the most common and the most growly.

That would be just her luck. A bunch of butt sniffing fur balls who'd think they could boss her around because she was, and had, a pussy.

Sniff.

Her inner she-Cat huffed at her vulgar description, but hey, she wasn't lying. Lucy was a hybrid she-Cat. A small, yet ferocious animal whose inner voice was as haughty as any high-class feline's.

Hmph.

For fuck's sake, she growled softly. Once again, she managed to piss off her beast.

Oh well. Suck it up, buttercup.

Ignoring her she-Cat's attitude problem. It took a moment, but her little beastie got over her feigned insult, and crept forward silently inside her mind. Lucy needed her extra senses to solve the mystery of who and what she was dealing with here.

"I said come in," the deep, gruff voice repeated impatiently.

This was definitely the man in charge. His brisk command was delivered with the practiced ease of someone used to being obeyed. Lucy took a breath and was immediately struck by a myriad of emotions, picking up on his sheer dominance, the scent of his fur, and a spicy male musk that made her inner feline freeze and take notice.

OMG. He brought me to the Alpha.

Lucy exhaled, fiddling with her hair as she battled her rising hysteria. She was mainly a solitary creature and pretty low on the totem pole of the

Shifter hierarchy. She rarely got to see the head honcho of even a small Pack. Lucy pushed the door wide, curiosity burning inside of her.

Standing with his back—*his broad, heavily muscled, and totally naked back*—towards her, the room's only inhabitant remained perfectly still. He was even bigger than Cole—maybe six and a half feet or more—at least a foot and a half taller than Lucy.

His hair was longer, brushing his wide shoulders in thick, dark waves. Physically, he was devastating, tall and built, biceps showcasing intricate tribal tattoos. He wore tight jeans and leather biker boots, and nothing else. The stranger practically oozed power and sex appeal. He was a total badass, and Lucy practically swooned, taking him in from the top of his dark head to his large, booted feet.

Holy hell. His arms were bigger than her thighs, and that was saying something. Both bore full sleeves of beautifully detailed tattoos showing a variety of scenes from full moon runs to a flock of birds rising over a stand of trees that ended with a pair of wings flapping high on his neck. She wondered what he would do if she walked on over and traced them with her fingertips, or tongue.

Eeek! Where did that thought even come from? Lucy knew better than that. Alphas did not dig submissive little nobodies like her. But no amount of self-deprecating thoughts could stop her from looking. There was no harm in that, was there?

It took only a moment, but she was reeling from the sheer masculine beauty of the man. She couldn't make out the words inked across his skin, but she wanted too. Wanted to touch, to smell, to kiss. She had a thing for guys with sexy hair, and his was black as pitch, like motor oil, and just as glossy.

An image of those wide shoulders, and that inky dark head bent between her legs had her shivering in the quiet. Shit. She needed to get her mind out of the gutter. Bad enough she was even feeling this way at all, worse because he would know. Freaking Shifter sense of smell would pick up the tiniest change in her body chemistry, including the ones that corresponded with arousal.

Every single survival instinct she'd honed screamed at her to get out of there, to run far away, but she remained rooted to the spot. Like some magnetic force was drawing her to the big, sexy as hell man. Finally, he turned, and she realized he must've spoken.

Oopsie.

Embarrassment caused her face to heat, but she refused to duck her head or shy away. She met his steady gaze despite the almost overwhelming urge to avert her eyes and bare her throat. Between the heaviness of his natural Alpha dominance, and the sudden, persistent throbbing ache between her legs, Lucy could hardly breathe, let alone think straight.

"Uh, sorry, what?" She managed between suddenly dry lips.

His black eyes flashed gold as he cocked his head in a way that reminded her more of an animal than a man. He was positively gorgeous, with chiseled features, kissable lips, thick eyebrows, a day's worth of scruff on his cheeks, and eyes that glowed inhumanly at her. Lucy couldn't take her eyes off of him.

"Who are you?"

"I'm Lucy Corwyn," she whispered back.

A deep rumbling growl came from his throat. His eyes turned completely golden as he swept her entire body with his gaze. She noted the deep, dusky tan that made his skin look like sculpted bronze. Probably from years on the open road. She'd seen his leather cut with the DWMC #55 patch on the back and surmised this was not only a Pack, but a motorcycle club too.

Swallow.

Was there anything sexier than a Shifter on a bike? Warmth spread throughout her limbs and her she-Cat purred deep inside her mind's eye. By the time the stranger opened his perfect lips to respond to her statement, her heart was pounding inside of her chest.

What was he going to say? His name? She bet it was something cool like Michael or Damien. Her imagination as running wild, but a girl had to do something to entertain herself when she lived mostly alone. Lucy liked to spin yarns in her head about strangers she'd see on the road. It helped quell the loneliness.

Pity, he would be just another stranger passing through her life. But that was how things were for Lucy. That's how they had to be, for her safety. So Michael or Damien was probably Bill or Ted. Her imagination was always better than the reality.

He cocked his head to the other side, his body practically vibrating with the force of his growling, and oh my gods, that sound was doing something crazy to her inner cat. It was like he was casting some strange spell on her without any words. She wanted to beg him to speak already. To end the madness churning deep within her. Then he did it. He finally spoke. One word only, but with it, Lucy felt her whole world turn upside down. The husky syllable fell from his mouth like liquid honey.

"Mine."

His voice had gone even deeper, if possible. Lucy bit back her groan. His scent had surrounded her, and it was like nothing she'd ever breathed in before. Her she-Cat hissed and purred, then yowled so loudly, she actually winced.

"Um, what?"

"Mine," he repeated, stalking her slowly across the room.

Lucy backed up against the wall, cursing herself for being dumb enough to get trapped. Her pulse increased and heart raced as his natural, wild musk *—like open road and well-oiled leather, hot and clean and so damn sexy she felt her panties dampen*—filled her nostrils. The cat growled at her to get closer, to rub her body all over the big mountain of a man—*not man, Wolf*—but she held herself still. Barely.

No. No. No. NO!

Yes, her cat insisted.

Lucy's eyes flashed, her animal pushing to be let out. Her inner feline ready to go belly up for Mr. Big and Hunky.

Slut, she hissed at her beast.

Mate, replied the wily she-Cat.

Dammit. She couldn't believe this. The enormous, sexy, tatted out Wolf was her mate.

"Fuck me," she murmured, and was shocked when the man pounced over the desk and pinned her to the wall.

"Anything you want, you just have to ask, baby," he growled into her ear.

Lucy closed her eyes and tried to ignore the throbbing of her sex as it instinctively prepared for his invasion.

No. Hard no.

She pushed against his impressive pecs and shook her head firmly.

"Whoa there, big guy. Back up a step," she murmured and pushed again, but it was like trying to move a mountain.

"You smell so good," he growled and nipped her earlobe, sending another wave of moisture dripping down her panties.

Lucy moaned. She needed to get away from him before she did something really stupid. A cold shower would work. Yes. She needed a cold shower to get her head on straight.

"Hey," she growled. "No means no, buster, now back up!" Eyes narrowed, she gave him what she hoped was her *I mean business* face.

The stranger backed up a half step but kept his frying-pan-sized hands firmly on her waist. Lucy exhaled and tried counting to three. She knew what guys like him were like. Big, macho, bossy, and sexy as hell. They were monsters in the bedroom, wrecking a woman for life by getting her addicted to him. Then he would leave. They always left.

Sexy he might be, but he was a Wolf and an Alpha, and she was just *her*. No matter how much her inner kitty begged, Lucy knew better. Acting on this would be a huge mistake. She needed to work to make money to fix her ride, then she was out of here. Surviving was her gig, not shacking up with a bored Wolf.

"Your skin is so smooth," he murmured in that deep, growly voice, drawing circles with his fingertips on her waist.

When had he hiked her damp t-shirt up? Dammit. She wanted to grab his hands, but if she let go of his chest, she knew he would be right back to smushing her against the wall.

Yes, please.

Her she-Cat was so down for that. Lucy shook her head.

No. Big fat double no.

"I said, back the fuck up," she growled.

This time, he allowed the full force of his smile to

spread across his ridiculously handsome face. His grin widened, and he took another, larger step back.

Come back.

Shut it, kitty.

"I am here for a job, not to be manhandled by some oversexed puppy," she snapped.

"Puppy?" The cocky male snorted.

"You're right. Puppies have better manners. You can't just push women into walls with your big, muscular body, you know," she told him, halfway to panic city.

"My apologies, mate. You just caught me off guard," he replied, arching one perfect eyebrow, grin still in place.

"Fuck this fucking day," she mumbled, then began to pace.

Her brain was going a mile a minute. She needed to try to get her thoughts under control, but first a little ranting was in order—in her own head, of course.

What in the ever lovin' hell just happened? I just came in here for a damn job. Stupid freaking car! Always breaking down. Now this? Really? He called me mate. Mate. For fuck's sake. He is my mate. My animal thinks so, yeah, but she is a horn ball. Besides, he can't be mine.

Is he a Cat like me? Nope. He's a freaking Wolf. A huge, hairy, bossy, thinks he's all that, Wolf. FML!

"Um, darlin'? You wanna take it down a notch? And I'm not that hairy," he said, slightly annoyed.

Well, damn. So much for an inner rant. She'd said all of that out loud.

Double oopsie.

Lucy straightened her spine and turned to look at the tall, gorgeous Alpha Wolf.

"Look, Fido, there's been a mistake—"

"Oh, I don't think so, darlin'."

Cocky. So fucking cocky.

Lucy had always had a secret thing for bad boys, and this guy was the motherfuckin' head honcho of bad boys. But was he really her mate? She knew all the Shifter myths of fated mates and true love and finding yourself in one other person created solely for you by the universe itself.

But she'd never really believed in them. It certainly never happened for her mother. Hope was a terrible thing for someone like Lucy, but right then, it was brewing inside of her like the beginnings of a storm.

If he was the storm, would Lucy be the calm? She wondered, really wondered, and for a minute, hell, she wanted to find out. Was she brave enough to stick around? Curiosity was a particular downfall for her kind, but one thing was certain, she would not be bossed around by this guy no matter what the Fates decided he was to her.

"No mistake here, darlin'. You're mine," he said, that sexy growl was back, and she shivered in response/

"Well, I don't think so. And my name isn't darlin'," she muttered.

"Alright darlin', how about baby instead?"

"It's Lucy, My name is Lucy. And you are?" she asked.

"Lucy. I like that. My name is Derrick, Derrick Rand," he replied, and reached out to shake her hand.

Fuck. His name was sexy. Not Bill or Ted, then. Dammit.

Lucy did not stand a chance in hell of surviving this.

"Oh, no you don't. No touching," she yipped, pulling back her hand at the last second.

She knew better. As worked up as they both were, if sexy Derrick here got his hands on her, it would be seconds before they started going at it like rutting beasts. As a feline Shifter, Lucy had to worry about going into her heat cycle only a few times every few years. But when presented with a viable male, one who claimed she was his, her cycle could start at any moment. Chances were, this meeting would have her coming into her heat in a matter of days.

Shiiiiit.

"Fine, darlin'. No touching *yet*," he murmured.

"Ever. Unless I say so," she countered.

And that will be never. She amended inside her head. She did not want to touch him. That would only start the mating fever even sooner. She'd been getting away with every three or four years since puberty, but she knew the stories. Once a female she-Cat Shifter found her mate, her ovaries basically exploded.

"Whatever you say, mate."

She could tell he was a cocky bastard from the arrogant tilt of his head to the way his knowing gaze seemed to undress her right there.

Yes, please. Too many clothes.

Down, girl!

Lucy was not ready for this. She turned to him with her eyes narrowed and hands on her hips and said the only thing she could think of.

"This isn't going to work. I don't want a mate."

CHAPTER 4

Derrick sat behind his desk and finished inputting the newest invoices, using the software system Phoenix had developed to help them run *Serious Moonlight* smoothly. Once he clicked pay on this last invoice, that would be it. All of their suppliers would have a zero dollar balance on their accounts. He clicked the button with a move of his wireless mouse and sighed.

Satisfaction thrummed through his veins, and yet Derrick's Dire Wolf growled inside of him. For some reason, his animal was on edge. He stood up and walked around to the huge shelf he'd claimed as his.

It was part of the original office, but like so many of the things they'd found here, had been left to rot. After stripping and sanding it down, he replaced two of the shelves, refinished the whole thing after salvaging it from the same mildew and mold that had sunk into various parts of the building.

A lot of the original furniture had been repurposed by him and his crew. Thank the gods they were all strong and good with their hands. But that's what happened when you lived your entire lives on the road. They'd picked up this and that along the way.

Of course, he'd started investing their money a few decades back and managed to increase their accounts. He'd used that money, plus a big chunk of his own funds, to buy this place. Looking at them, people probably figured they had little more than a pot to piss in, but the opposite couldn't be any truer.

The Pack accounts were healthy and fat. Added up, they made a nice, round eight figure number spread out across the globe. Personally, Derrick's account was of a similar status. But he was a man of few needs, and material things were never that important.

Money never mattered much to him. It was a means to an end, not the end. Not for him. He'd lived too long to not know what was truly important in this world.

Derrick may look a little over thirty, but he was

triple that age. His Shifter abilities included living a much longer life than humans. Sometimes, they outlived other Shifters as well. It was a Dire Wolf thing.

His own mother was over three-hundred-years old. Still alive and kicking, leading her own Pack of twelve widowed she-Wolves who preferred to live honoring the memory of their mates by riding their bikes cross country the way they had when they'd been together.

It was sad and beautiful. Tragedy plagued those destined to live after their loved ones passed into the next adventure. Derrick had worried about leaving his mother when he'd decided to branch out on his own with a few Wolves, but she'd slapped him on the side of the head affectionately and told him to stop cramping her style. She was a good mother and had assured him she'd be just fine. After all, she'd taught him how to ride. He still blushed at the memory, but he'd only been a kid and she was so strong and wise. His mama sure had taught him a thing or two on the back of his first Harley, and he was damn proud of her.

His Wolf paced and grumbled inside him, feeling unsettled and anxious. Fuck. This was something the bar was supposed to calm in him. Derrick wiped sweat from his brow. Suddenly, he was hot in the tiny office. He ripped off his black t-shirt and leaned on the shelf, allowing the air from the vent to cool his overheated body.

The Wolf was getting aggressive, pushing, and snapping at his skin, demanding to be released. He knew settling in one place was going to be a challenge for his Pack, but he'd forgotten his own animal might not take to it right away. It would take some time, he supposed. And that was something he had plenty of.

Fuck. He felt really *really* hot now.

It was like his blood was boiling. Not in anger, though. More like anticipation. A knock sounded on the door, and he listened to one of his own speak. Someone was there for the job they'd been advertising.

Finally, he thought, relieved. Sheila had been bitchin' about getting more help and here was a guy applying for the job. It was a little late, but who was he to judge.

"Send him in," he grunted, not bothering to turn around.

His Wolf would tell him if he was in danger from a threat. Derrick closed his eyes and listened to the footsteps of the stranger. They were lighter than he would have guessed. Much lighter than a Shifter male, even a regular human male.

He sniffed the air, sorting through the harsh chemical cleaners and paint that still hung in the air from their massive remodeling of their bar.

A female?

After his initial shock, he breathed again. His Dire Wolf had gone silent, the hunter inside him weighing the threat of the newcomer. His heart rate increased as the beast found something else in that new fragrance. Something intoxicating and terrifying in the female's scent. It was heady and dangerous, and very, very tempting.

Derrick sucked in a deep breath and held it in. Her scent was light and woody, fresh as spring flowers and just as uplifting. Like that moment you step off your bike after a seventy-two hour straight run, taking in the life bursting all around from the sunrise to the insects, the birds, and even the weeds on the side of the road. The scent invaded his senses, and he took a moment to savor it as his pulse sped up inside of him, thundering like a herd of wild stallions. That crazy, beautiful, wild scent seemed to wrap around his limbs, shooting straight for his cock. The damn thing grew thick and hard in his already tight jeans. He ached and throbbed, his Wolf growled and scratched, urging him closer to the source of that amazing smell.

Fuck.

Need pulsed through him, making thought almost impossible. He breathed again. The woman was calling to him, and he hadn't even seen her yet. He tried to steady himself before turning around. His Wolf was riding him hard, but Derrick did not want to scare her. He should take a minute, try to assess the situation.

Sniff sniff.

Feline Shifter. Sexy little kitten. Mine.

It didn't matter that she wasn't a Wolf. All he cared about was how fucking fantastic she smelled. Derrick growled deep and low in his throat. The sound reverberated through his chest. The near thousand pound animal inside of him urged the man to turn around and take a look. He asked her who she was, and waited, but she didn't respond. He needed a name to go with that scent.

Derrick turned, eyes flashing with his beast. "I said, who are you?"

Eyes the color of wild spear thistles met his, and he knew. Right then and there. This woman, *sniff,* this she-Cat was his. His one true and fated mate.

After that, it was a matter of self-control. He'd

finally managed to get his hands on her, couldn't seem to stop himself, he had to breathe her in up close. Once he'd recognized her as a Shifter, he figured it was all going to be fine, eventually. Surely, she would rejoice. The same way his heart did at the thought of finding his one true and fated mate.

She had a momentary panic, and he waited patiently for her to get through it. Discovering your mate could be shocking. And she was so fucking cute, pacing and shaking her pretty little head as she ranted. But imagine his utter and complete shock when she'd turned around and refused him.

"I don't want a mate."

Derrick recoiled inside as if she'd slapped him, but he didn't allow her to see it. Nope. Yes, it sucked. She wasn't as overjoyed as he was, but he didn't let that get him down. This sassy little feline was all his. She just didn't realize it yet.

"Lucy, we can talk about the mate thing later. Why did you come here?" he asked, openly curious.

"I need a job so I can pay for the repairs to my car and a place to stay for a little while until it is fixed. Then I'm leaving," she said, not quite meeting his eyes.

His Wolf snarled at the thought of her leaving but reined in the animal. He wanted her to choose him, but he would not get that by bullying her. If his life had taught him anything, it was that in order to play the long game, you had to be patient.

Derrick could be patient. Even if he wanted to tear her clothes off, make her come until she was screaming his name, and begging him to mark her with his bite, he would hold off. Wooing the sexy little feline was going to be fun, he mused, determined to make her so crazy about him, she would never want to stray from his side.

"So, you need a job and a place to stay. How come you came here?"

"Tony the Perv said this place was a boarding house," she explained.

"Who the fuck is Tony the Perv, and where can I find him?" Derrick asked. He couldn't help the growl that entered his throat.

Why would she call someone a perv unless he was acting pervy? That was just totally fucking unacceptable. He knew by the way his Wolf snarled that his eyes were full on gold with his beast, but he couldn't help it.

The sound of his pretty little mate snapping her fingers in front of him brought his head up. Her violet eyes were glittering as she did. Damn, she was hot when she was pissed. Derrick growled deep in his throat and a wicked hint of a smile grew on his face.

"Hey, knock it off, Fido. Quit the grumbling, he didn't touch me. Besides, I mean, *hello*, I'm a Shifter. I can handle myself."

"But you call him the Perv?"

"He was just a creepy little human. He didn't do anything to me. Anyway, I'm fine," she said.

That she was reassuring him without realizing it made his insides warm and his beast rumble in satisfaction. She was taking care of him, sweet, sexy, thoughtful mate. And she was right. She was a Shifter and a badass. As long as she was happy, so was he.

Damn, that was fast, but that was the way it happened. Derrick felt as if he'd been struck by lightning. His entire body was wound up and tense, but he couldn't let her see that. He wanted her calm and relaxed, ready to accept his claim. He just had to work on the *when* part.

"Alright," he said. "I will let it go."

It wouldn't always be the case. He was bound to be pigheaded and overprotective, not to mention possessive as fuck, especially once he claimed her, but he could see that she was perfectly fine. Good for Tony. The Perv would never know how close he came to being mauled by a pissed off Dire Wolf. Still, his beast wanted him to sever the man's head from his body.

Bashing heads and taking names was kind of an old, favorite pastime. His other half could be a bit bloodthirsty. Just another Dire Wolf thing.

The prehistoric animal had some very black and white notions of what was acceptable and how to deal with what was not. Mostly, what that meant was something or someone was bleeding at the end of the day.

Derrick had yet to be on the receiving end of such dealings, but he'd dished out his fair share of bruises and broken bones. Of course, he tried to limit his maiming to the really bad fuckers. Which is the category he'd put anyone in who tried to fuck with his mate.

Mine. Grrr.

Did he mention he was a possessive asshole? Well, yeah. It would only get worse the longer he went without claiming her. Mating fever could take him if he didn't get a handle on this now.

"Lucy, I understand you came in here looking for a job, but you know what we are to each other. I know you can feel the pull," he began.

"And I know what you'd like to *think* we are, but I

am telling you, the Fates made a mistake. I'm not looking for a mate," she told him firmly, shaking her head and looking him dead in the eye.

Dammit, if he didn't find it hot as hell, he'd wonder if she was challenging him. Derrick was not used to anyone showing so much indifference to his dominance. She had spirit and spunk, and fuck, he was intrigued.

He narrowed his eyes, but she held his gaze. Derrick was an Alpha. Not many people could hold his stare. Okay, no one had ever held his gaze for more than a few seconds, but there she was, staring him down, and his Wolf was preening like a lovesick fool.

"Lucy," he said, testing the weight of her name on his tongue, and finding he liked it very much.

"I know my name. What's yours again?" she inquired with that certain haughty air only felines had.

Fuck it, he shrugged, finding he kind of liked it. Haughty looked sexy as hell on her.

"Derrick Rand," he replied immediately, unable to resist trying to please her.

Goddammit.

He was acting like a lovesick puppy already. The

notion should've pissed him off, but he couldn't help grinning.

"Well then, Mr. Rand—"

"It's Derrick, darlin'," he drawled.

"Fine. Derrick darlin'," she teased, rolling her pretty purple eyes. "Do I get the job?"

"Yes," he said automatically.

"And the room?"

"Yep, that too," he smiled.

He did not relish the idea of his mate working in the bar, but it was the only way. He wasn't so pigheaded he couldn't figure that much out. Derrick had to keep her there with him, otherwise how could he claim her? And claim her he would.

"Come on."

"Where?" she asked, not completely trusting him.

Good girl, being careful with a stranger. But Lucy was safer with him than anyone else on the planet. The sassy little feline didn't know it yet, but she was. His dire Wolf had already claimed her in his mind.

"Grand tour," he growled and held the door open, staring at her ass as she sashayed in front of him.

Sexy little kitten.

Derrick walked her through the bar, out the door, and to the Pack house. It was dark and cool outside, middle of the night and all, but he was sweating bullets. He frowned as he looked around.

"It still needs work, but we are on it," he told her, wanting her to like the place.

"It's fine. The house is huge," she replied as Sheila came bounding over.

"Hi, I'm Sheila Rand. And please tell me my cousin hired you," Sheila screeched, stopping just short of plowing down his tiny mate.

He couldn't help his warning growl. Sheila yelped, and his mate's cute little head popped up. She glared at him, treating him to eyes that blazed purple fire.

"Really? Down, Fido," snapped Lucy in his direction before she turned to smile at his cousin.

"Hi, my name is Lucy, and I'll be working here for a couple of weeks till my car is fixed. By the way, your cousin has some serious issues with personal boundaries."

"Does he now, Miss Kitty?"

Sheila lifted both her eyebrows and whistled long and low. Derrick was not amused.

"What happened to your car?" Sheila asked, ignoring his warning growl.

"Broke down. It's a hopeless old junker, but it's mine. Car repair shop says it's going to be sixteen hundred dollars to fix, but the tow truck driver said you all ran a boarding house?" she asked, biting her lower lip, and making his dick go even harder.

Shit. She really shouldn't do that. If his mate wanted nibbles, Derrick was her man.

"We don't run a—*er*, yes, I mean, we do," Sheila said, wincing.

"Knock it off," she snapped again, and he cut off the growl he did not even know he was making.

"See what I mean?" she asked Sheila.

"Boundary issues?" his cousin replied with a teasing lilt to her voice.

Shit.

"Yep, loads of them. Anyway, to answer your question, *yes*, I got the job, and now I'd like to go to my room—"

"Cole," bellowed Derrick, turning his head to the door where the Wolf came running.

"Call the local tow company and have them bring Lucy's car here. When it arrives, fix it."

"Hey! That is my car, and it stays where it is," Lucy snarled at him, and fuck if he didn't find that hot too.

"*Ohmygods*," Sheila yelled, and jumped up and down excitedly. "Please tell me you are for real!"

"Uh, yeah, I am real. I mean, I am standing right

here," Lucy replied, head cocked to the side, staring at his cousin like she was daft. A sentiment he echoed at the moment.

"Derrick, I can't believe you found your mate already!"

"Who said anything about a mate?" Lucy asked, her voice getting all high and squeaky.

"Yes, Lucy is my mate," he stated aloud, and fuck, it felt good to own that.

"Damn cousin, you lucky SOB. But why do you always have to show everyone else up?"

"Ugh. Not you too," Lucy argued. "Look, I am no one's mate! I'm just gonna work here and get my car fixed."

"Cousin, she's awesome. Congratulations," Sheila said, jumping up and down and clapping like she used to when she was a kid and something excited her.

"Alright, Sheila, yes, you guessed it. Lucy is mine, but we haven't discussed any of the logistics yet," Derrick told his cousin.

"Oh, I see," Sheila said, still clapping.

"Hello? I am right here. And no, Sheila, for the record, I am not *his*, I am not anybody's. Look, I am tired, and wet from the rain, so how about you show me to my room, please?"

His sweet-tempered mate ignored him as she sashayed across the lot and through the narrow path to the gate and pushed the door open. Derrick growled softly in his throat. He nodded at Sheila, who seemed to understand his orders without words, as she usually did.

Out of all of his Wolves, she was the most intuitive. His sweet Lucy turned around one final time and gave him the stink eye. Fuck, her eyes were so pretty. A blue so deep, they were indigo. Purple eyes, blonde hair, sexy as fuck curves covering her petite frame.

Damn, she looked good. He'd never expected a sassy little kitten was his future, but now that he'd met her, Derrick couldn't imagine it any other way. This was definitely going to be an interesting mating. Derrick's Wolf howled in his mind's eye, the huge beast clamoring to be closer to her.

Mine. Mate.

Soon, he told his animal, *soon*.

CHAPTER 5

Lucy inhaled the fresh evening air outside her new job at *Serious Moonlight*, grateful to finally be outside.

Yes, the night before, she'd slept like the dead. Her inner feline had felt safe and secure for the first time in a long while. What that said about her circumstances, she did not want to look too deeply into.

The room she'd slept in was just fine. Clean and spacious. Okay, she'd been given the best damn room in the house, a fact that made her wary. It took her all of a minute once she'd stepped inside to recognize it was *his* room.

Fury had filled her, and she'd wanted to hunt him down and castrate the heavy handed bastard, but her inner kitty would have none of that. The dumb feline thought it was sexy and romantic. The big bad Wolf wanted her—*a cat*—in his Den, surrounded by his scent, where he could protect and watch over her.

Prrrr.

She'd readied herself to be strong against the wooing she'd felt coming, but to her surprise, he'd stayed away. Confusing man. He'd insisted they were mates, set her up in his bedroom, with his things, but that was it. With a hurriedly whispered goodnight, Derrick had left her alone in his space. He didn't even ask her to come in.

Not that she needed him inside to know what he was doing. His heady musk covered every damn surface, driving her she-Cat wild with need. Screw him and his restraint. She was feeling unfulfilled and angsty after her restless night.

Fine. She was horny. Really fucking horny.

Lucy had thought he would have tried knocking on her door in the wee hours of the morning, playing on her weakness for him, but nope. He'd given her the space she'd asked for.

Stupid overbearing, Alpha.

She replayed the events of the night before in her mind, trying to find fault with him, but couldn't.

"This is your room, isn't it? No, I can't stay here—"

"Look, if putting me out of my room bothers you so much, I could stay," he'd murmured and stalked her until she'd backed against the wall. "I want to stay, Lucy, but I think you need some space to wrap your head around this thing between us."

"There is nothing between us," she'd argued.

"So, you don't need space, then?" he'd teased, cocky bastard that he was.

Lucy had wanted his hands on her, and as if he could read her mind, he'd smoothed one long-fingered hand down her arm, skimming over the skin, conjuring goosebumps across her flesh, but barely touching her at all.

That whisper-light touch had almost been her undoing. She'd wanted to press against him. Something of a feat for a woman who prided herself on control. Truth was, she had little real sexual experience. Her mother had flocked from man to man and Lucy refused to get caught up in that cycle of use and abuse.

Still, her she-Cat urged her to rub her skin all over his mountain of a body and mark him with her scent. She resisted. Barely.

"You wish," had been her reply before stomping out to the delicious sound of his laughter.

Of course, she'd left his room with yet another pair of wet panties on the pretense of using the bathroom. Thank goodness they had a washer and dryer in the house. She had one backpack that held her clothes, and laundry day was every day for Lucy. But her meager eight pairs of panties were going to be threadbare if this kept up.

If this kept up, she was gonna buy stock in *Victoria's Secret*, for fuck's sake. She'd managed to avoid him for two days. Only saw him at mealtimes, which was uncomfortable, but doable since she was often hungry enough to focus solely on her food.

The blond Beta of the Pack was a real chef. His Texas chili with juicy, thick chunks of beef, and homemade jalapeno cornbread, were outstanding. She'd expected Derrick to make a stink of her, refusing his invitations to join her for walks and evening runs in the woods behind the house, but he didn't. Took her refusals in stride and never stopped watching her.

Was he waiting for her to cave? Maybe. Lord knew she wanted to. Hell, her she-Cat wanted her to. But each time he asked, she turned him down flat. Lucy couldn't explain it.

Her body said *go get him girl*, but her mind said *be cautious*. She could not believe he had anything other than a quick roll in the sack in mind, and the thought terrified her. If ever a man was made who could wreck her body and heart, it was Derrick Rand. Maybe he was counting on wearing her down, but she was no easy mark. No matter how worked up he made her, or how desperate for his touch she became, Lucy needed to keep strong.

I will not end up like Mom. No fucking way.

Being afraid sucked, but there it was. Lucy was no match for a big, strong Alpha. She was a scaredy cat. No pun intended.

She'd do anything and everything to avoid the inevitable heartbreak fucking around with Derrick Rand would bring. She did not know how to separate love and sex. Had tried it once in her teens. She'd given her virginity to her high school boyfriend, but idiot that she was, she'd fallen for the guy. They grew apart and went their separate ways, and fuck, it had hurt.

Lucy was in no rush to experience that pain again. Only this time, she knew it would be a hundred times worse. She was not a kid anymore, and her loyal heart would be well and truly damaged if she gave it to him. She could not afford it. Staying away from Derrick was her only option.

Good thing work kept her busy. Tonight was

opening night, and Lucy had spent the afternoon cleaning and making sure the bars and kitchen were fully stocked along with the rest of the Pack. She'd been introduced to them all over the last forty-eight hours and was amazed at their very existence.

Dire Wolf Shifters. Who knew?

At least she was not the only female, even if Sheila wasn't exactly warm and friendly. At least, the female wasn't a bitch either.

Another dog joke, she mused. They'd been trading cat and dog jokes almost nonstop with Sheila calling her Mr. Whiskers, and Lucy leaving an old tennis ball she found in the parking lot by Sheila's door. No matter how far the female tossed it, Lucy always found it and brought it back.

Snort.

The men were pretty distant with her, but that probably had more to do with Derrick introducing her as his mate than for any personal reasons. Lucy gritted her teeth just thinking about his unwarranted proclamations.

"You aren't going to bully me into accepting your claim, Derrick," she'd told him, but the big, sexy male just grinned.

"I'm no bully, darlin'. I'm an Alpha willing to do anything to keep you happy, safe, and secure. You'll see. I

won't stop until you do," he told her, and that had been the first time he kissed her.

A quick press of his lips against hers. She'd been so shocked Lucy hadn't moved a muscle. No response, no rebuttal, she just stood there stone still. The touch was gentler than she'd expected, and brief. Too brief.

Want. Need. More.

Dammit. He wasn't going to seduce her. Not for a quickie and certainly not into accepting his claim either, for fuck's sake. Lucy was her own person. Once upon a time, she'd once dreamed of having a mate to love, who loved her. Someone to build a home with, complete with white picket fence, cubs —the whole nine yards. But that was a child's dream.

Lucy was a woman now. After her mother's last lover had cleaned out her bank account, even the coffee can that held a few random twenty-dollar bills, the female had simply wasted away. She'd died on a Wednesday, leaving Lucy with a week left till graduation, and nothing but the clothes on her back.

Lucy had stayed to get her high school diploma, then she'd taken off. Her mother was buried in a pauper's grave, and it shamed Lucy still to know she could not have given her any better. She'd had to skip out on the landlord, not having the money to pay the rent.

All alone to fend for herself in the big, bad world at just eighteen. It took her a year to save the two hundred bucks and mail it to that old man, but she did. She had her pride, after all.

Her father had never really been in the picture. She didn't know how to contact him and wasn't sure if she would have, even if she did know. Some Shifters just didn't stick around. She'd had years to get over her abandonment issues, but repressed feelings had a nasty way of resurfacing now and again. Pushing back the hurt, Lucy took a deep breath and went over what she knew.

Derrick Rand was the Dire Wolf Alpha, head of their MC, and he'd announced to all and sundry that she, Lucy Corwyn, hybrid feline Shifter, belonged to him. His mate.

Crap.

What did she know about how Wolves mated anyway? And really, what the hell was a Dire Wolf? Some kind of mutant gene had led this subspecies of Shifter to maintain their prehistoric animal, long since extinct in the natural world. She was curious, but she wouldn't ask questions. She didn't want to get involved. No matter how much her she-Cat yowled and hissed at her. Lucy was simply not going to budge on this.

I don't want a mate.

She kept on repeating the mantra inside her brain, telling herself she believed it. But if that were true, she had to ask herself why she couldn't stand to be in the same room with Derrick for more than ten minutes at a time.

True, he was an Alpha, and power seemed to ooze from his pores when he walked into a room. But Lucy was not frightened of him, nor did she feel compelled to obey him. On the contrary, his inner strength, that special Alpha magic he had, turned her on like nothing else ever had.

She loved his inky hair and the way it fell to his chin and brushed his shoulders in dark waves. Her fingers itched to brush the constant shadow that seemed to always cover his chiseled features, making him even more outrageously gorgeous than seemed fair. He hadn't kissed her again, but the curve of his smile and the heat in his eyes made her want to climb him like a mountain and slam her mouth to his.

Rrrr.

Going to his room after cleaning the bar to shower and dress did nothing to cool the fire in her blood. Lucy felt her heat coming on, and it worried her something fierce. If her animal had her way, she'd be wearing Derrick's claiming mark already. She tugged on her uniform, grinning at the shirt Sheila had dropped off earlier that evening, as promised.

Lucy had laughed out loud when she'd seen it. Clearly, Sheila was trying to get her laid. Her so-called uniform was nothing but a pair of tight, high-waisted cutoffs that showed a little too much of her ass cheeks. Two Wolf paws were painted on each back pocket in hot pink. That alone would undoubtedly draw eyes to the bottom half of the ensemble.

As if that was not bad enough, she'd paired it with a skin-tight, black tank top that left the tops of Lucy's creamy rounded breasts bare. Across the front of the shirt was the *Serious Moonlight* logo, written in a brash, hot pink scrawl with a glowing white, full moon above it. The moon sat right on her left nipple, and made Lucy laugh even harder.

On her feet she wore a pair of black leather, mid-calf harness boots that she'd picked up at a second-hand store during her travels. They'd been barely used and too good a deal to pass up. Glad now that she'd grabbed them, even though they cost more than she'd ever spent on shoes before.

Living on the road meant little opportunity to make money, but she'd always managed. Her she-Cat was agile and hearty, enabling her to do physically demanding jobs when need be. Though she was short, and a fair bit curvier than most Shifter females, Lucy was happy with her body.

This outfit left more of it than usual on display, but she was comfortable with herself, and it would be easy to work in. Thank goodness she'd shaved. If her shirts were any shorter, her *hooha* would be hanging out.

Snort.

Bad enough her skin was pasty and pale, white as milk. She'd have liked having a tan to at least give the appearance of slimmer thighs, but it was what it was. Most customers would probably not be looking past her cleavage, which was pretty impressive if she said so herself.

Big boobs, big ass, thick legs, hell yes, Lucy was the real deal when it came to being curvy. She liked her body and did not mind flaunting it. So, take that, assholes of the world who thought all women were supposed to fit into the same size pair of pants!

Truth was, she'd never stuck around a man long enough to find out if her body was a problem. If Derrick had anything to say about the way her rounded body filled out the stupidly skimpy uniform, then he could go to hell. She pulled up short, realizing with a gasp that she was nervous about him seeing her like this.

When the hell had it ever mattered to her what a man thought about her looks? Eyes narrowed, she decided to grab her wobbling self-confidence by the horns. She was not gonna stand outside and worry about anything as ridiculous as whether her mate— no, not her mate, her boss—liked it or not. He picked the damn thing out, after all.

"Dammit," Lucy muttered to herself as she pulled open the heavy double doors and sauntered into the bar with the wind blowing back her thick, blonde hair.

She'd taken time to blow out her long locks to a glossy sheen. Yeah, the rumors were true, Cat Shifters were really into their fur. Lucy was proud of her golden locks and her plus-sized shape. She'd taken extra care tonight with her makeup, too. She'd put on liquid eyeliner and mascara, some glittery shadow on her eyelids, and a smear of gloss over her already pink lips.

The place fell quiet the second Lucy walked in. It was half an hour till opening, so it was just the guys and Sheila, but still. Lucy looked up to see several pairs of glowing eyes staring at her, beneath them, mouths were hanging open.

"Wowza! I wasn't sure you'd wear it," exclaimed Sheila, before running over to grab Lucy in a girl hug.

The redheaded beauty wore a similar outfit, only her legs were tan and about a mile long, and her high, perky breasts seemed to stand up and salute. Sheila held Lucy's arms wide, eyeing her body in a mock-leer that had Lucy giggling.

"You look great, girl. My goodness, you are gonna get so many tips!"

"Oh, please, look at you. You're like runway model gorgeous," Lucy replied sincerely.

"Damn, ladies," said a Wolf with red hair two shades darker than Sheila's. His name was Weylin, and he'd been quiet but friendly to Lucy over the past two days. "We're used to this one here, but Lucy, you look good enough to eat!"

Similar comments and a long wolf whistle sounded just before a menacing snarl came from the back of the room. Everyone shut up and Weylin backed away, hands raised in surrender. His glowing eyes were averted, and he bared his throat in deference to his super pissed off looking Alpha.

"It was a compliment, man. No disrespect intended," Weylin ground out, throat still bared.

She'd seen Derrick staring at her with his eyes glowing gold, that angry rumble still coming from his throat. Instinctively, she stepped forward, shoulders back, head high. So much for being nervous about him seeing her this way. Her inner kitty lent her some much needed cool, and she approached him with the slinky gait of her kind. Sex and confidence dripping with each step as she got closer to him.

He liked what he saw. She could tell by the wicked gleam in his eyes and the bulge in his tight jeans. Fuck, she really liked the way he wore his jeans, perfectly molded to his muscular thighs and calves. Lucy bit her lip, watching as he tracked the movement, but she didn't slow down.

Derrick tensed, as if waiting for her to stop, but Lucy had other plans. She walked right past him, not stopping until she reached her post at the bar in the back room. Of course, she could not help but shiver when she passed him by, noting the heat that seemed to radiate off his skin.

"Back to work," Derrick told the rest of the males, who seemed stuck where they'd been standing.

Lucy had to work hard not to grin stupidly. Truth was, she enjoyed rattling the big, bad Alpha. It made her feel powerful, knowing he couldn't stop staring at her with all the intensity of a hunter stalking his prey.

"What are you wearing?" Derrick's voice asked from just beside her ear, and she realized he'd snuck up on her while she'd been checking the coolers.

"My uniform. Sheila gave it to me," she replied.

"Fuck. We don't have a uniform, Lucy. If we did, it would have more material," he muttered, and ran a hand through his hair. "Go throw something else on."

"What?"

"I said you don't have to wear that."

"No, you said I should 'go throw something else on'. What I want to know is why me? Sheila's been in here for hours, and no one said a word about her outfit. But suddenly, I show up, wearing the same thing, and it's a problem?" Lucy's voice was growing louder by the second, but she couldn't help it.

"Lucy—" Derrick growled, but she did not let him finish. Not this time. Lucy was pissed.

"Is there something wrong with my body? Too many rolls and jiggles for you, Mr. Muscles? Is that it?"

"What? Fuck! Lucy, of course not—"

"Is there something showing I should be ashamed of? Or would you prefer I wear a tent to cover my fat?" Lucy demanded, angry and shaken that he had been so serious in his command.

"Dammit, Lucy! Fuck, no. That's not what I said or meant. Here, come here," he growled and took her hand, tugging her down the hall.

She was so angry she went without hardly a fight. Her heart was pounding so hard it was liable to explode from all the hurt and rage. She hardly had time to think about what she was going to say, let alone how to react to the way he quickly pushed her up against the wall the second he closed the door inside his office.

Derrick was vibrating with his own emotions, his ever present growl filling the space and turning her on so much, she wanted to die from embarrassment. Damn him for making her want him, even when he was clearly ashamed of her.

His hard, muscular body pinned hers in place. She felt the thick ridge of his cock pressing against her soft belly, and she couldn't stop the whimper that escaped her lips. His face was so close she could smell the peppermint he'd sucked on after they all had dinner an hour ago.

"Feel this?" Derrick growled and ground his lower body against her belly.

Oh yeah.

She felt that.

Holy. Fucking. Giganticock.

"I'm harder than I've ever fucking been, Lucy. My dick is aching like a fucking virgin in a strip club, for fuck's sake, and it's all because of you," he growled, chest heaving as he tried to regain control.

"What—*why* did you say that then?" she asked, voice so low she hardly recognized it.

"You look fucking beautiful, Lucy, and I'm losing my mind with wanting you. My Wolf is going wild with the need to claim you, and I am trying, Lucy, I swear to fuck I am. But the longer I wait, the more possessive I get," he grunted.

"I can't help it. I'm trying, but I'm bound to fuck up a thousand times a day."

"So, you don't think, uh, I look bad in this get up—"

"Fuck, no. Never. You are the sexiest female I have ever seen. I fucking love your curves, Lucy. You were made to fill my hands, and I got big hands, darlin'," he said, and she could hear the truth in his deep, growly voice.

He was so damn hot, so masculine and forceful,

and he was being real with her. She could hold herself back when he was being bossy or cocky, but when he was being honest, fuck, he made her eyes cross with need. His tone was rough but held an edge of pleading to it that made her want to swoon at his feet. It was enough to make all her pink bits throb with desire.

"Look at me, Lucy," he told her, his long fingers catching her chin when her eyes would have dropped.

Forced to meet his midnight gaze, Lucy trembled in his arms. Derrick blinked again, his eyes glowing with the gold of his Wolf. For the first time, she took stock of the beast peeking out at her, and what she saw was stunning. His Wolf was a wild and untamed beast. A prehistoric monster full of dominance and power. The animal wanted her, wanted to sink his teeth in and claim her, and the only thing holding him back was Derrick's human side.

The sheer force of his will was what kept her from being claimed already. He was waging an internal war with his animal, and all for her. Nothing had ever touched her so deeply as knowing what this man was doing for her. Shit. She was being selfish. Fate was not something easily denied, and his animal was clearly stronger than any she had ever encountered. If nothing else, that told her loudly and clearly what kind of man he was.

Good. Strong. Honest. True. Caring. Loyal. Trustworthy.

Derrick's whole body seemed to tremble against hers, and she automatically reached out to cradle him. He was vulnerable with her, in that moment, and maybe that was when she first started to fall for him. Like really fall for him. Big, sexy man, letting her see his soft side.

The raw need on his face plain, and fuck, she felt it too. Lucy swallowed hard. Was she hurting him as well as herself by neglecting his claim and their growing bond? Maybe she was wrong to deny what she already knew to be truth. Derrick Rand was hers every bit as much as she was his.

"Lucy," he whispered her name and pressed his forehead to hers, holding her as if she were something precious to him.

"No one ever really stuck with me before," she said, feeling the need to explain a bit of herself to this beautiful, strong man. "I didn't grow up with an abundance of love and security. My Dad walked out when I was a kid. Mom died after a string of boyfriends left her broken and bruised. If this is real, Derrick, I'll need a little time to get used to it, to get used to you being here," she whispered, hating her past.

"It's real. I know you need time and I'm trying to give it to you."

"I know you are," she whispered, petting his chest and shoulders, loving the rumble of pleasure that rattled through him at her touch.

She was not lying. This would take some getting used to. If Derrick really was her fated mate, she'd have to accept him and his claim. She would have to open herself up to hurt. That part was scary, but worth it, right?

Yessssss.

Her she-Cat hissed in righteous joy as she acknowledged the truth, even if only to herself. Derrick's nostrils flared, and he groaned, closing his eyes as he unconsciously flexed his hips against her. Was it wrong that she found it sexy that he was struggling with control?

She couldn't help it. Having his body pressed up against hers was doing things to her she'd never felt before. Desire pulsed in her blood, catching like wildfire in her veins. She could hardly breathe, definitely couldn't talk anymore.

Her lips parted as she tried to suck in air. A whimper escaped her, or was that a sigh? Fuck if she knew. Her body was on fire. Lucy moved slightly, nuzzling his nose with hers, their breath mingling.

"Just a kiss," she murmured, and he nodded, dipping his head, and pressing his mouth so softly against hers it barely registered at first.

She pushed her tongue into his mouth, needing more, and he gave it. Damn, did he give it. The man was a god at kissing. His teeth nipped, tongue stroked, and lips brushed against hers until she could no longer think clearly.

Derrick grunted and lifted her up. Lucy whimpered, wrapping her legs around him like some crazy, clingy octopus. Her heated core rubbed over his bulging jeans, stroking her needy clit just right.

It wasn't enough, though, not nearly. Lucy could have cried, she wanted him so much. The scent of her desire grew thick and heavy, and Derrick flared his nostrils. His chest vibrated with a slow, deep growl that seemed to shoot waves of lust straight to her sex.

"You got me so damn crazy, woman," he growled, kissing her deeper as he pulled her tighter against him.

He felt so good between her thighs. She moaned and allowed him to move her just so. Every brush and stroke had her Cat closer to the edge. The man was so damn strong, holding her with no effort at all. Every pant and groan made it harder for her to think. She'd almost forgotten why they were in his office to begin with.

"Do you know why I wanted you to get changed now?"

"No," she murmured, chasing his mouth for more kisses, but beast that he was, he denied her.

Fucker.

"It's cause I'm a possessive asshole, darlin'. These curves," he growled, cupping her ass with one hand, and reaching for her tit with the other, "are mine. The idea of dozens of eyes on you has my Wolf tearing at my insides. I'm greedy and I don't share, but you have nothing to hide or be ashamed of, woman." He paused a beat and she let his words sink in.

Holy. Fuck.

He was breaking down walls with words. Destroying her armor and making a mess of her well-laid plans.

"Look at you. Fucking goddess. I want to rip those shorts off your body and bury my cock so deep inside you, you won't know where you stop, and I start. I don't want another fucking person to see you and be tempted to touch, cause I don't know if I can stop my Wolf from going after someone tonight," he continued.

"Derrick—"

"No, kitten, let me finish so you understand what kind of man I really am. I am protective of what is mine, and bite mark or not, you're mine. It's just a matter of time—"

"Cocky bastard," she butted in, but she was grinning.

"Yes, I am. And you, you are perfect. Every fucking inch of you is a thing of beauty. Now, I spoke too quick before, and I am sorry. A real man doesn't tell his woman how to dress. He lifts her up and compliments her. Tells her how good she looks and how she makes him feel. Well, Lucy, you look better than anything I have ever seen, and you make me crazy with wanting you," he confessed.

She was caught in the golden stare of his Wolf, and she wondered who was in control at that moment. Since he was still holding her, and she was not bent over his desk being claimed by his rutting beast, she figured the man was still in charge.

What Lucy could not figure out was whether or not that fact made her happy? Derrick's control was immeasurable at this point. But did she want the big brute to keep it or to claim her already? Her she-Cat had already decided. The Bobcat-Mountain Lion Hybrid inside her knew what she wanted.

Mine. Mine. Mine.

"I make you crazy?" she asked.

"Fuck yeah, you do. Every delectable inch of you has me wanting to be inside you so damn bad I can't think of anything else. Far as I am concerned, we're mates, kitten. My Dire Wolf is jealous as hell, but I'm keeping him at bay. The fact you won't let me claim you is making him feral. I almost attacked Weylin back there just for commenting about how you look in those *fuck me shorts* you got on and he's been part of my Pack for five decades."

"You guys are old as fuck," she stated, and he barked out a laugh.

"Maybe, but I've never seen anything that compares to you, darlin'."

She swallowed at his confession. Loved the power she felt having brought his animal so close to the surface, but at the same time her she-Cat longed to soothe him, insisted she tend to her mate.

Lucy ran her hands across his perfectly sculpted shoulders in the soft, black button-down he wore over a plain white t-shirt. He was so damn big. Big enough to make her feel positively small, even though she knew better. She totally loved it.

"You're playing with fire, kitten. Keep petting me and I'm gonna take what you're offering. I can't help it. Want you so bad," he said, eyes closed in an almost painful expression.

Lucy cupped his cheeks in her hands, offering him what they both wanted, and Derrick did not hesitate. He opened bright gold eyes and pinned her with his stare before dipping down to capture her lips in a soul-searing kiss. All Lucy could do was hold on and let it happen. His lips were soft yet firm, demanding but tender, and so damn hot she could have come just from having his mouth on hers.

Her she-Cat yowled inside her mind's eye. The little beastie was happier than a pig in the mud because she finally had her mate in her grasp. Lucy purred and lapped at his lips, sighing when he opened for her and tangled his expert tongue with hers.

He was all spice and heat. His flavor unique. A mouth-watering, smoky combination of forest and peppery fire. She couldn't get enough of him.

Lucy growled and nipped his lip, delighted by the way he tightened his hold on her ass and face. His claws extended, and she felt them pierce through her tiny jean shorts, but he didn't break the skin there.

Not yet.

The hint of pain made her she-Cat hiss and growl in pleasurable anticipation. The feline wanted her mate to mark her, to claim her, here and now, but Lucy was not ready for that. Not yet. Her stomach clenched and pussy throbbed.

Dammit. Her heat was coming, and fast. But not tonight. It was close, the mating fever almost had her, but not quite yet. She had some time left, time to get to know him. Things were moving at light speed, but that was the way for Shifters. She knew that even if she did not understand it.

Lucy had a decision to make. One that would change her life forever. Derrick's gruff voice interrupted her thoughts as his lips left hers and skimmed her jawline and neck. It felt good, so good, when he nibbled her there.

Just like that.

"Will you wear something of mine? Something to carry my scent. My shirt? My watch? Fuck," he growled, moving back to her mouth and shaking her from her sweet, lust-filled thoughts.

"Will it help?"

"I think so. I can't promise I won't go after the next fucking person who sees you like this tonight without you wearing my mark," he told her, and she heard the truth in his words.

His voice dripped sex and power, a heady combination Lucy found irresistible. She knew he was talking about hurting someone for looking at her, and were she a regular old human, that might have made her nervous. But Lucy was a Shifter. She found his possessive attitude as sexy as she did exasperating.

Shifters were notoriously territorial. She might not have accepted his claim verbally, but they both knew it was a matter of time. She bit her lip and looked at his glowing gold eyes.

"You want me?"

"You know I do," he replied.

"You really want me?"

"Fuck, yes, woman," his voice sounded rough, full of his Dire Wolf.

"Then you're gonna have to prove it, Fido," she said, licking her lips as she slid down his body till her boots hit the floor.

"How?"

"You might be the Alpha, but if I'm your mate, that means I'm one, too. Your Alpha fem. Is that right?"

"Yes. Mine," he grunted.

"Then you're going to have to trust me. Let me live my life, Derrick Rand, Dire Wolf Alpha. Back off and believe me when I say that I can take care of myself."

"It's not an easy ask—"

"I know. That's why it will prove you're the kind of man I can be mated to," she said. "I want a partner, not an owner. I want a man who appreciates me and makes the effort to understand me."

"I'm the only man for you, Lucy Corwyn," he clarified.

"Good. Now, you just have to prove it," she told him and winked before walking out of his office.

If this thing had any chance of working, then Lucy needed him to know she would not be bossed around. She had to be his equal. Sure, it was tempting as hell to just bend over and let him claim her, but she'd witnessed firsthand what happened when sex was used to manipulate a person. Lucy would not fall prey to her own desires.

She wanted Derrick more than she wanted air, but Lucy wanted this to last. She had one shot at making a life with him as his mate, and she was going to fight damn hard to make sure they made it.

She demanded respect. Needed independence. Craved companionship. Wanted to be wanted. And then there was love. She'd never believed in it before, but something about Derrick Rand had Lucy hoping for that one particular miracle.

Mates were supposed to be for life, and Lucy was not about to settle for anything less, regardless of what life had taught her.

Meow.

At least her she-Cat agreed.

CHAPTER 6

Derrick frowned hard at the sixth fucker who walked up to the back bar, eyeing Lucy like a hungry hyena coveting a lion's kill across the wide expanse of wood before placing an order.

Motherfuckers.

Why the heck had he ever promised to let her take care of herself tonight? She had nothing to prove to him. He knew her she-Cat was fierce and bold. But she was his, dammit. He wanted—*no, he needed*—to protect her. Wanted to provide for her. To keep her safe and secure.

It was ingrained in his DNA, for fuck's sake. He watched as she smiled at the *soon to be dead* asshole, waving a crisp fifty-dollar bill at her while ordering his drink. The dickface tipped it towards her, almost brushing the filthy bill across her ample cleavage, but she snatched it before it made contact, and turned her back on him while hastily stuffing the bill in the tip jar by the cash register.

Good mate. Strong as hell woman. Badass Shifter.

Derrick grinned as he watched her return with the man's drink in hand, and Lucy's brilliant white teeth flashed between her plump pink lips. Immediately, Derrick's thoughts went south. He imagined that mouth wrapped around his cock, how hot and wet she would feel sucking on him. Fuck, he went cross-eyed at the image. He had to adjust his cock in its tight confines. Ordering himself to stop picturing all the things he was going to do to her incredibly fuckable body the second she said yes.

Please be soon.

The strap of her tank top fell off her shoulder as she bent to grab a beer from the cooler for another customer. What the hell was Sheila thinking with those outfits? Obviously, the stack of bills tossed inside the tip jar was what.

Grrrr.

When he'd first seen her in that tiny excuse for a uniform, he almost lost his fucking mind. He knew she was beautiful, had thought so from the second he'd laid eyes on her. She was so petite compared to him and curvy as fuck. Pure sex appeal packed into five-feet, six-inches of purple-eyed passion.

He'd never seen eyes like that on anyone, and Derrick had been around the block more than a few times. Lucy Corwyn was a fucking bombshell with her rounded ass and full breasts, tiny, indented waist, and long, smooth legs.

Her straight glossy hair was thick and dark only at the roots like fresh ground coffee beans, then lightening to gold and platinum at the ends. Her eyes fucking amazing and her mouth, hell, if he thought about that now he'd spend the rest of the night doubled over. Then there was her scent.

Holy. Fuck.

She smelled like heaven to Derrick, light and woody like that perfect moment in a quiet forest just before the sun broke out over the canopy. Sweeter than cherry pie, warmer than a shot of whiskey, his sweet, sassy mate smelled like home to Derrick, and for a Dire Wolf just learning to put down roots, that really meant something.

His beast wanted to roll around in her scent until it covered him. He wanted to stamp himself all over, make sure everyone knew she was taken. She was the perfect culmination of everything he'd ever fantasized about in a female. Strong, sassy, funny, tough as nails, with skin soft as satin, and eyes that floored him.

Her kisses started fires in his blood, and when he'd pressed his body to hers, Derrick was delighted to discover they were a perfect fit. Of course they were. He was dying to really find out, though. Could not wait until they were together, really together.

With anyone else, sex was a formality, a physical need, an urge. With her, it was so much more. Attraction, yes, but it was more than her perfect tits and round ass that called to him. It was her soul, her heart, and that quick witted mind he wanted.

Life was not always kind, and his sweet Lucy had been hurt before. Derrick was going to cherish her, covet her, tend to her every need. He was going to earn her trust and thank the gods every day for delivering her into his arms. She made him want to control his beast. Made him want to be a better man.

For her. Always her. Only her.

Every cell in his body was attuned to her already, and he hadn't even claimed her yet. Licking his lips, he tasted her on the air and frowned as another fucker raised his hand to get her attention. The man's eyes were too greedy, his leer too familiar.

Shit.

Derrick could not afford to blow their opening

night by losing his temper. Even Shifters drew the line when it came to fighting in public places. He was blowing hot and cold, his mood changing from wanting to claim his heart-stopping mate, to wanting to murder every single asshole in the bar who even dared to breathe the same air as her.

Grrr.

Fucking fuckety fuck. That skimpy uniform left way too much of her on display. That was it. Derrick was going to kill his cousin for giving Lucy that damn thing. *Fine*—maybe not kill—but he was damn well going to eat every box of whatever fruity cereal his cousin was most likely hoarding in their kitchen. Little she-Wolf thought no one knew they were there because she always double-wrapped them in freezer bags and aluminum foil, but Derrick was a motherfucking Alpha. His sense of scent was superb.

Not only would he snag a bowl for himself, but Derrick was going to tell Cole where they were, too. The younger Wolf loved cereal. Another customer leaned over to whisper into Lucy's ear, and Derrick almost went berserk. His eyes were glued to his mate's perfect face, while every fucking dickhead in the place was staring at her body.

Fucking Sheila.

The she-Wolf definitely did this shit on purpose.

He really needed to calm down. The animal was riding him hard, claws popping out every few seconds, and it was all he could do to hold on to his skin while standing there.

Focus on the bar, he told himself.

But his Wolf would not allow him to stray far from Lucy's station. Doomed to failure, he tried looking around to see how the others were progressing. The animal was keen on protecting his territory and his people.

The crowd was good. The local Shifters had sent a fair amount of their kind to see them get started, and as promised, he gave a ten percent discount to all Shifters tonight. The Shifter Council had sent him the names of some local Shifter-run businesses, and they'd responded with generally welcoming replies. Some even promised to send some customers his way. Normally, he'd be looking forward to chatting with a few of their customers, but he was too distracted. The need to mark his mate was overshadowing reason, testing his control to the limit.

He could hardly fathom how she had kept him at bay for two whole days. He'd been worried when she claimed she did not want a mate at all. So fucking glad she'd changed her tune to *prove you want me by trusting me.* Not that that shit was any easier. As if trusting her was the problem—ha! It was the rest of these fuckers Derrick didn't trust.

He turned his head and inhaled a good, deep breath, filtering the different scents to try to get a read on who, *and what,* were occupying his bar. He noted a few Bears from the nearby Barvale Clan, a few Macconwood Pack Wolves, including the men and women in the band he'd hired for the night, and a couple of Tigers from the Maverick Pride.

Sniff.

Mostly, the crowd was comprised of Wolf Shifters. Regular Gray Wolves, not Dire, but those existed in abundance in New Jersey, so that was to be expected. There were also the odd Fox, some Coyotes, a Stallion or two, and was that a Hedgehog? The local Vampire Clan was asked to give the Shifters their space, but Derrick had promised them a *ladies' drink free night* for the following week.

As he took in the crowded room, pride filled him. They'd done a good job with renovations. Every inch of the place gleamed with polish and new paint. The industrial style roadhouse looked both modern and classic, with the newly refinished beams now on display after they'd ripped out the godawful popcorn painted ceilings. Derrick was quite fond of the huge wooden beams and the large iron screws, nuts, and bolts that were now visible.

Coupled with the old barn doors they'd found and repurposed to act as partitions between sections, the gleaming refinished oak floors, and the new paint job, the place looked incredible. The sturdy old bars had been on the verge of destruction in the dusty old relic of a roadhouse before they'd saved them from the mildew and rot that had started to infect them both.

Thor had taken a particular liking to the one in front and insisted they find a way to keep a lot of the original furnishings. Derrick had wondered at the time if it would be worth the huge amount of work, but he was glad he'd went with his Enforcer's suggestion.

They just didn't make bars like that anymore. The original craftsmanship was something to truly wonder at. Plus, they were large and built for use, which was exactly what a bunch of Shifters needed. No dainty glass-topped tables for *Serious Moonlight*. This was Shifter country, even if the normals had no idea. Built to withstand a bunch of rowdy Shifters out to let their hair, *er*, fur, down.

They'd all agreed that the atmosphere should invoke fun, promote social interaction, and give off a generally good vibe. Of course, they expected fights to occur now and then, but it would not be the focus of their establishment. This was their home now.

They installed standing tables only around the dance floor, where a raised stage, featuring the band, had been redone with expert lighting and sound equipment courtesy of their resident tech geek, Phoenix. You could sit and eat, but the dining area closed at ten. After that, there were a couple of dozen stools surrounding the main bar if you wanted to sit and have a drink. Another two dozen were at the back bar.

Where Lucy was stationed.

His mind flitted back to his sexy little unclaimed mate. *Don't go there yet,* he warned himself, and took another wide sweep of the room. Every surface was either gleaming wood, metal, or had a fresh coat of matted cream or black paint. Plain, simple, and neat.

Of course, their logo was another story. Almost garish, truth be told. The bright neon pink sign Sheila had designed and ordered, without asking anyone's opinions, had taken a huge chunk out of the Pack's accounts, and was, of course, non-returnable. Brock and Weylin liked it just fine, thought it added some fun to the otherwise severe appearance out front.

Derrick supposed they'd never get a lot of women inside if the only thing greeting them was the two dozen gleaming Harleys they'd put on display outside. Thor, their acting bouncer, stood at the door, able to keep an eye on the bikes and the crowd easily. Should anything happen, Derrick had absolute faith that he'd notify the rest of them immediately.

His eyes continued sifting through the crowd. Lots of talking, smiles, and drinking, which was good. Drinking meant money, and that meant success. Derrick used a bit of his Alpha powers to locate his Pack mates and the Wolf inside him breathed easier, knowing his people had this.

He watched Sheila work for a little bit. His baby cousin was one hardheaded woman. She'd had a miniature neon *Serious Moonlight* sign made up for behind the main bar, and it was glowing in the otherwise dark atmosphere, washing everything in pink and making everything more appealing somehow. He smirked at her know how.

Combined with the t-shirts and tank tops carrying the logo that she'd insisted the bartenders and cooks wear, Sheila was becoming something of a marketing genius. They were even selling modified t-shirts to customers, and he saw at least three big Bear Shifters wearing them already.

The front bar was crowded with people, normals and Shifters alike, Every single one of them clamoring for drinks, food, or just some attention from his Pack. Sheila worked with a steady hand and a ready smile with Weylin at her side.

Derrick nodded at them, then his gaze traveled, landing on Thor's tattooed, bald head, standing high above the rest. His bulk combined with his almost black eyes, bronzed skin, and close-cropped beard made for one scary as fuck bouncer. Perfect fit for a New Jersey roadhouse. His real title was Enforcer, and Derrick couldn't have chosen a better man for the task either way.

Next, he found Phoenix and Cole on opposite ends of the place. The two were working the crowd, dressed in their best jeans and button downs. They'd insisted they would look more like managers without the pink logo t-shirts. Derrick had agreed, much to their undying happiness and Sheila's annoyance. But they were doing a bang-up job, ushering folks with drinks to empty standing tables and helping other customers to empty spots on the dance floor. Cole was taking food orders back to Brock, his Beta, and head chef. The scent of barbecued wings, ribs, and burgers tinted the air with delicious, savory spices.

"Just enough of an aroma to tempt them to order." Brock explained when installing the expensive and truly excellent ventilation system.

All his people were working together to make this a success, and Derrick was so fucking proud right now. The future looked good as hell from where he was standing. It was what they'd been doing, what they'd done best, for all those years on the road together.

He knew a few of them were unsure about this place, wary of settling down in Blue Valley, but Derrick felt it in his bones. This was it for them. This was home. And that feeling had only grown stronger the moment he'd met Lucy.

Two days had passed, but she was already fitting in with his Pack. She'd joined them for meals and engaged in playful banter with the gang. He'd been nervous about that, worried she might feel uncomfortable being a hybrid she-Cat amongst Wolves. He had yet to see her beastie, and he had to admit, he was dying to do just that.

His gaze flicked over to where she was working, tending bar, and he noticed her laughing at something a customer was saying. She looked good enough to eat with her purple eyes flashing and pink lips tilted up in a welcoming grin. Lucy tossed her head back as she laughed, and her thick, glossy waves made her look like an angel. Unfortunately, he also noticed her customers' eyes flick to the large amount of cleavage on display and his Wolf tensed.

Grrrr.

Eyes narrowed, he walked over. There were more men than women, but that was usually the way with places like this. Roadhouses were notorious for fighting and carousing. Sure, he wanted their place to be known for other things. Like having the best, coldest beer on tap, the highest quality whiskey on hand, and the most delicious, freshest food cooked on site by a professional chef, with live music every night of the week.

However, if that smooth-talking fucker with a death wish didn't stop flirting with his mate, Derrick was going to put *Serious Moonlight* on the map as the first roadhouse in New Jersey to host a vicious murder in view of an entire fucking barroom full of people within three hours of them opening the door.

Mine.

Lucy snuck a peek at Derrick from across the room. He'd been watching her all night. A fact she found as disconcerting as it was sexy. His quietly persuasive, alarmingly powerful aura was unlike any other Shifter's she'd ever met. She knew all too well that males, especially Alpha males, could be a possessive bunch of assholes—to the point of suffocating the happiness right out of a relationship.

Cat Shifters were loners by nature, even if for her, it was more a circumstance kind of thing. Still, she found herself wanting more from life now that she'd met Derrick Rand. Even his name was sexy. Bonus points to him for not letting her down on that front. Could this work?

She'd been mulling it over for two days now, and

in Shifter years that was like a month at least, right? The man was an Alpha seemingly loyal and fierce, and even better, he wanted her.

He. Wanted. Her.

No one had ever wanted her as their own before. Not as a friend. Not as family. And certainly not as a mate. She'd been skirting the actual claiming, but even without his bite, she felt the weight of his promise to make her his. His golden eyes followed her, and Lucy's heart sped up so much she thought he must be able to see it pounding through her skimpy little tank top. The bastard grinned, nostrils flaring as if he could smell her need from all the way over there.

Cocky much?

Hell yes, he was and surprise, surprise, Lucy liked it. In fact, she liked just about everything she'd learned about the huge, tattooed male. It was difficult for her, trusting strangers, especially men. Allowing herself to feel safe long enough to create bonds was something she did not think would happen easily for Lucy. And yet, it was happening now. She felt her chest tighten and squeeze when she thought of this Pack and this place.

Typically, she'd be planning her escape right about now. But Lucy did not want to go. Maybe she was warming up to the idea that Derrick was her mate, even if he was still basically a stranger.

We could remedy that tonight.

Her inner beast pushed the thought into her head, and dammit all, she was actually considering it. She could seduce him. It would be easy. He would let her. Yes, he'd already made sure she knew he meant business. But what did she really know about him besides the fact that he was a Dire Wolf Shifter and a biker.

Was he really willing to settle down or would he take off and leave her first chance he got? Her animal was tickled with the idea of having a mate and cubs—furry little traitor purred with delight every time she saw him or felt him near. But her human side was still uncertain.

What did fear ever get you?

Lucy bit her lip. It was too fast, but she knew that's how it happened sometimes. For the lucky ones, anyway. But when had she ever been lucky? No. Screw that. Lucy stomped down those negative thoughts and focused on pouring beer and whiskey. Reading the label on the bottle in her hand, she smirked.

Of course, a Shifter bar would have *Bite* on hand. The handcrafted artisanal whiskey was distilled by

Mason Lane, a Wolf Shifter over in Maccon City. Lucy had heard all about him from some Wolves over in the seaside town a few summers back. She'd been passing through, as usual.

Always looking in from the outside.

Morbid thoughts were not welcome tonight, so she pushed it aside and made the next drink. Lucy approved of the label. *Bite* was some damn fine whiskey. It came in several flavors and had fun little names to go with. Now she poured a second shot of *Winter Bite* into a glass for her customer. The guy was with a friend, a relative probably, and they were both sinfully good looking, but Lucy found she only had eyes for one Wolf.

One very large, pretty pissed off Wolf, who was heading her way, looking like he was about to break something or someone in two. She turned her head to the two good-looking strangers and winced. Someone was about to have a new asshole torn in his backside.

"Thank you so much, babe. I think maybe you should gimme your number so we can talk, hang out, what do you say?" the guy asked.

Lucy sniffed. Oh fuck, this was not good. The man was Wolf, and he was leaning over the bar. Too close now, but he was a smart fucker, cocking his head as he read her tank top aloud.

"Serious Moonlight? Catchy name."

"Yeah, it is. Um, stay on that side of the bar, please," she responded noncommittally.

"Oh yeah? That an insurance thing?" he asked, winking at his buddy while he tapped the bar for her to pour another round.

"Uh, yes? I mean, probably," she muttered, following Derrick's angry stride.

Fuck. Fuck. Fuck.

"You're new to town, right? Come on, babe, gimme your number," he said, giving her a wide grin that must have melted hearts wherever he went. The dog.

"Yeah, I came into town a little while ago, but no on the number. Sorry, pal."

"Can't date your customers, huh? You know, this is a nice place and all, but I know another bar you can work where that sort of thing is allowed. Want me to make a call, I will, babe."

"No, thank you. I'm fine."

"You sure, cause I think you're missing out—"

"Everything alright here, Lucy?" a deep, familiar voice asked.

"Fine, Derrick, thank you," she replied, eyebrows raised.

She could see his control wavering and had to applaud his attempts to follow her request to allow her to handle things herself. The stranger took one look at Derrick's bright gold gaze and dropped his shot on the table like it was hot. She could not blame him. Dominance rolled off him in waves, even the humans who did not know Shifters existed seemed to want to move away from him. Fight or flight instinct was a real thing, and anyone with half a brain felt the urge to run from Derrick Rand.

"Enjoying yourself?" he growled the question at the Wolf.

The stranger narrowed his eyes at Lucy, then tried to meet Derrick's stare, but dropped his gaze after three seconds.

"Uh, yeah. You are?"

"Derrick Rand. I run things here."

"Oh. Nice. We heard you all were settling down," the Wolf said, looking uncomfortable as he tracked Derrick's golden gaze to Lucy, then back again. His buddy idled up to him, a blank expression on his face.

"Hi, I'm Jordan. This is Zeke."

"Nice to meet you, I'm Derrick. This is Lucy."

The silky, deep, possessive notes in Derrick's reply had hit a cord straight in her heart. The *my* before her name was implied, and she couldn't help the quick twerk of her lips upwards at the thought. The way his golden eyes washed over her had her heart beating double time before he turned and settled his stare on the now grinning stranger.

"Looks great in here," the Wolf named Jordan said. "I work at The Thirst Dog over in Maccon City. My boss wanted to wish you all good luck, but he's home with the wife and kids tonight. Family game night."

"Tell him thanks. Have a beer on me?"

"Sure, bro," Jordan grinned.

Derrick asked Lucy for three beers, and she grabbed some cold long necks of a good, old fashioned American lager, no crafty IPA shit.

"Cheers," Zeke mumbled, lifting his beer to his lips.

He gave Lucy one sad look, like she was this missed opportunity, but she just shrugged. Her heart belonged to someone else, and it was about damn time she faced it. The three Wolves remained at her station while she served other customers, and she couldn't help the thrill of knowing Derrick remained close to her because he wanted her. It was quite a feeling, being wanted. Lucy liked it.

A pretty and sophisticated looking woman sauntered up to the trio, placing a possessive hand on Jordan's shoulder. With a knowing smile, she turned that pretty face to Derrick, and fuck, Lucy was not prepared for the size of the green-eyed monster that roared to life.

"You must be Derrick Rand," the woman said, offering him her hand.

She was a very pretty woman. But Lucy's jealousy was totally unnecessary. Her name was Isa, and she smelled like magic. She was also Jordan's very claimed and very happy mate.

Nice.

"I have to tell you, this place is freaking awesome," Isa said.

"The Thirsty Dog is pretty exceptional too, but it has a different vibe. As does Bar None in Barvale. Between the three of us, I think we'll be giving folks like us some diversity when it comes to hanging out and letting loose. Besides, a little healthy competition is good, don't you agree?" Jordan grinned at the question.

"I can see that, but how would we track how we're doing?" Derrick asked.

"Well, Wade Kettle, he's the owner of Bar None, and Mike run a monthly poker game. Sometimes trusted staff joins in, like me, and we talk shit and talk cross promoting each other's places. It's a lot of testosterone and horse foolery, but it clears the air and settles the animal, if you know what I mean," he murmured.

"I do, thank you. I would be happy to join."

"Awesome, I will tell Mike."

"Thank you for a wonderful time," Isa said, waving to Lucy who nodded at the stunning female.

"Yeah, man, good luck with the new place and, uh, other things," Zeke muttered, looking miserable.

The Wolf was not smiling as much as he was earlier, but he still dropped a fifty on the bar, and gave Lucy a wave that he cut short once Derrick growled softly in his throat.

Beast of a Wolf. But so totally hot.

The three Macconwood Wolves stood to leave, and Lucy lost track of Derrick for a moment. The bar was busy, flooded with new customers, and she had work to do. She moved about, flipping bottles and catching them before pouring out drinks for the thirsty crowd. Shifter reflexes were awesome for this kind of thing. That and she wasn't tired standing on her feet for nearly nine hours straight. Her antics with the bottles earned her a few more twenties in the tip jar. But she frowned at the growing pile.

Weird. She should be thrilled. Lucy needed the money to fix her car, but the idea was to leave once she paid for the repairs. Suddenly, that didn't strike her as a good thing.

Stay. Stay. Stay, her she-Cat begged.

"*Cocktail* fan?" Derrick asked.

Somehow, the giant man had managed to sneak up behind her after she'd finished pouring a couple of shots of *Cinnamon Bite* for a group of young Shifter females. Lucy half-smiled and handed the shots over to the trio, who did not bother to leave a tip.

Bitches.

"Hey there, handsome. Wanna do a round?" one of them asked Derrick.

Lucy was going to rip this female's head off if she didn't back the fuck up off her man. Derrick replied noncommittally, but that was not enough to sate her angry she-Cat. The young she-Wolves were all thin and good looking, eyeing Derrick like he was a chocolate buffet, for fuck's sake.

A snarl escaped her lips, and she felt her claws extend before she could stop them. Derrick placed both big hands on her hips and pulled her back into him. The feel of his hard, muscular body at her back calmed her inner beastie. She leaned back into him, loving the way his scent enveloped her. Her inner animal purred happily.

Good mate, offering us comfort and reassurance.

Lucy did not disagree.

"Um, yeah," she replied to his earlier question. "I watched three Tom Cruise movies on a constant rotation when I was a cub. All we had was this TV/VCR combo and only the VCR part worked. Mom got us the movies at a flea market," she replied, offering him some insight into her life.

If he really wanted her, he should know what he was getting. Lucy was not fancy. She was not educated past high school, and she had little experience at much except running. She was a hard worker, though, and she was honest.

Shame was not something she felt very often, and her past had never been in her control. She shrugged off him, uncomfortable with the way she missed his touch almost instantly.

"You sure about this?"

Lucy turned her back on him, determined to keep him from seeing the way he affected her.

"Lucy, I have never been more certain of anything in my life," he drawled in that deliciously low growl of his—*the one that seemed to always conjure moisture between her legs.*

Fuuuck.

Wet panties again. Just for that she turned around, pressed her body into him as she reached for a bottle of something behind him. Her breasts were smushed against his hard torso, and Derrick stiffened—*everywhere.*

For the first time, the Alpha looked unsure about what to do next. With a hint of a smile on her face, Lucy slowly raised herself high on her tiptoes, her nose brushed along the side of his neck, and she did something that shocked the shit out of her. She opened her mouth and bit down slightly, teasing him before turning quickly to pour a shot.

She didn't have a customer waiting. This one was just for her. And as she tossed it back, he grabbed her hips, slamming her back against him. Fuck, she loved this. Loved the feel of his big, strong body, his giant, hard as steel cock pulsing against her ass.

Somehow, he'd moved them over to the side where no one could see them, and she thanked the gods for it. Derrick's mouth was on her neck now, and she was purring, actually purring out loud at the feelings he was creating inside her body. They shot through her like lightning strikes. He was sucking on her neck in earnest now, a steady growl reverberating from his chest straight through her back. He was so much bigger than her, but somehow, they fit as he ground his cock against her ass.

Suck, lick, kiss, bite, bite, bite.

He was making her dizzy with his attentions, and Lucy loved every second of it. She wanted him so damn badly. Wanted his kiss, his cock, his bite. All of it. All of him.

Her she-Cat demanded she get her ass in gear. Pushing back against him, rubbing herself on the massive hardness she felt right alongside of her cloth-covered cheeks, Lucy told him without words she was ready.

Derrick growled with his mouth over her neck. He held her there before dropping the skin, kissing it gently and holding her close while he tried to gain control of his breathing. He stilled her movements with arms like steel bands, wrapping them tightly around her waist.

"You're driving me crazy, woman," he grunted and dipped his head, catching her earlobe with his teeth. He tugged on the sensitive skin, and she moaned helplessly.

"Fuck, kitten, if you don't stop those noises, I'll have you right fucking here in front of the whole damn world. I'll claim you now, Lucy, and an audience won't even slow me down," he growled, sounding tortured, and she stilled.

Shit.

He really was holding on by a thread, and as much as she wanted him, Lucy was not into fucking in front of crowds. Her whole body tensed with a need she had never felt for the big, warm, sexy Wolf. Heat seemed to exude from him like a furnace, wrapping around her and keeping her warm. The deep, powerful rumbling coming from his chest vibrated through her body, and she could almost imagine how good it would feel if he did that with his head between her legs.

"Be good," he grunted, and bit her earlobe again. She could hear the teasing note in his voice and breathed easier, knowing the real danger had passed.

"That was the most erotic thing I've ever felt, Derrick," she whispered.

"Keep on teasing me, kitten. It's gonna make things so much better when I finally claim you," he growled, and she heard the promise in his voice clear as day.

He bit her again, harder this time, but not enough to break her skin. Her animal loved the nip, and her body reacted to it as well, swelling with need, growing wetter by the second. She groaned as his tongue laved the spot he'd bitten, soothing the delicious hurt.

Lucy looked in the mirror behind the bar at the picture they made, hiding, and making out in the far corner. He was behind her, holding her like she was something precious, eyes glowing gold and chest rumbling with his beast. Tattooed arms held her, and fuck, was he sexy. His whole body was a work of art. The intricately detailed design of his tats uniquely beautiful. She wanted to trace each one with her hands and tongue.

Lucky Lucy. The Fates had given her a king, and in that moment, she wanted desperately to be his queen. She wanted to learn everything about him, memorize every inch of his body, stamp herself on his heart. She wanted to make him a part of her, become part of him.

Lucy froze, this level of intensity scared her. She'd never been this needy, this desperate for someone. Even so, that enormous wall she'd built around her heart so long ago seemed to crumble and crack a little bit more with every second she spent with Derrick Rand.

At this rate, she'd be bending over for him by the time they closed the bar. Then she would be at his mercy. He would have power over her no man had ever had, and Lucy was terrified. She wanted to move away from him, but couldn't go. Her last chance to save herself from the agony that had destroyed her mother was slipping away, and she was scared to death.

"I won't hurt you, Lucy. Let me satisfy you, darlin', we both know I am the only one who can. Tonight, let me claim you tonight," he begged.

Lucy closed her eyes, wanting to give in with everything she had. But what happened after? When he grew tired of her, and realized she was no match for a powerful Dire Wolf like him? The thought chilled her, and Lucy found the strength to push off him. His arms dropped, and he expelled a harsh breath. She was hurting them both and hated herself for it.

"No."

"Lucy—"

"No," she repeated, and nodded at a sour looking man who appeared to be waiting for a drink.

"Can I help you?"

"You one of them, aren't you? For years I been tellin' folks to watch the woods. We got animals here. People-animals. Like you," the nasty man spat in her direction.

He stunk of booze, fear, anger, and hatred. The combination hit her in the face like a slap, and Lucy flinched.

"Sir, I think you've had enough—"

"Ain't taking no backtalk from a stinkin' animal," he slurred. He was about forty with a heavy paunch and a week's worth of stubble. "Can't lie to me, girly. I worked as a guard for a top secret research facility until they canned me a month ago for taking some pictures home with me. Had to prove it to my wife, see," he mumbled, and Lucy backed up another step.

Secret research? Animals? Fuck, this did not sound good.

"Okay, mister, I think you better leave now," Lucy stated firmly.

"Yeah, you are one o' them, ain't you? I saw you letting that big freak over there grope you by the wall. You think I couldn't tell? Freaks, all o' you. Fucking animal whore—"

Lucy backed up at the man's violent outburst, but what really had her in shock was Derrick. He'd somehow vaulted over the bar and had the human by the collar of his shirt and off the ground. With one shake of his head Thor ambled over and took hold of the man.

"You think you can just come in town and take over with your sluts? Freaking animals! All of you!"

The man's yell was cut off by Derrick's threatening growl. A few customers had stopped drinking, watching the scene with glowing eyes and she exhaled as they made a wall around them. Keeping the Shifter secret was an important part of their world, but somehow this human had stumbled on them. Lucy did not know who needed to be called in, but if the government had research facilities involving Shifters, the Council should be told.

"What should I do with him, boss?" asked Thor.

The Dire Wolf was even bigger than Derrick, angrier, more menacing somehow. He was the biggest man Lucy had ever seen. Even so, there was no doubt about who was in charge. Derrick was the Alpha. He glared angrily at the drunk, then leaned over and whispered something into Thor's ear. The male nodded and took the drunk outside to be dealt with.

The crowd around them resumed their revelry, and the band played on. Most of the customers didn't seem to notice anything wrong. Folks were still drinking, snacking on wings and pretzels, and those on the dance floor kept on moving.

Good, she'd hate a fight to ruin their opening

night. This Pack had worked so hard and deserved to succeed. Lucy watched Derrick's back as he stood guard in front of the bar. She noted a few other men sneaking off, leaving almost immediately after that jerk had been thrown out, and she knew her mate had taken care of it.

Good Alpha. Good mate.

She wondered briefly what would happen to him, but trusted Derrick implicitly to keep her, his Pack, and their secret safe. Lucy could not afford to spend loads of time on it. She had work to do. People were thirsty and the crowd only got bigger, but nothing she couldn't handle alone. Not that she had the chance to find out, since Derrick wouldn't leave.

He stayed and worked right alongside her. A fact that surprised and pleased her, though she would never admit it. Every second together, the sexy Alpha was chipping away at her armor.

Chip, chip, chip.

"I can handle this," she whispered, knowing full well he could hear her even with the music.

"I know you can, kitten." Derrick winked. Lucy's irritation rose over his manhandling, but, if she were being honest, it kind of tickled her pink bits too.

Sexy, caring, protective man.

For the next couple of hours, they worked side by

side, taking orders, cleaning glasses, opening bottles. He was no slacker. She'd give him that. He kept the ice coolers full and did all the heavy lifting. He restocked the beer, carried another case of whiskey, and unloaded the dishwasher before she could ask.

Lucy's inner animal huffed a breath and rolled over where she rested in that metaphysical plane until Lucy needed her. It was clear then that her animal was done with her. Until her human half accepted the fact that this Wolf was her mate, her animal would be discordant.

Dammit. Was it getting hot in here?

She felt her temperature spike and her stomach tighten. Dizziness threatened to make her wobble, but before she could fall, she felt something firm and strong wrap around her arm. A second later, something cold and hard was pushed into her hand.

"Sit. Drink," came the crisp order, and Lucy's eyes narrowed.

She was not going to obey him like one of his damn Pack. He could take that glass of, *wait*, what was it? She opened her eyes against the headache that was beginning to form and looked down. Her rant stopped immediately. Lucy's heart squeezed, and she found herself fighting back a gasp.

Oh, no, he didn't. Yep, he did.

He'd poured her a tall glass of iced sweet tea with a curl of apple hanging from the rim. It was beautiful. It was perfect. It was her favorite drink. All the wind left her sails, and she sunk down on the stool he pushed underneath her.

"Take a break, kitten. The crowd's thinning out. I'll handle last call."

Well, damn, she thought, and brought the glass to her lips.

The cool liquid slid down her throat and quieted the fire that was starting in her blood. This was the first sign of her heat. It was coming on sooner than she'd thought. The question was, would she be strong enough to take what came with it?

Would Lucy be strong enough to let the Alpha of the Dire Wolf Pack claim her?

Yesssss, her she-Cat hissed.

Eeeep!

CHAPTER 8

Derrick frowned as he listened to his mate pacing around in the bedroom upstairs. A week had passed since the bar had opened, and as usual, they closed at three o'clock. Instead of staying to clean with the rest of the Pack, he'd left Brock in charge, and hauled Lucy on home.

Home.

The word sounded right, but his animal was not feeling it yet. It could be a real home at long last, if only the sassy little feline would accept his claim already.

Fuck.

He was losing his mind. Yes, she had only known him for a couple of weeks, but his beast knew the second he'd seen her, she was his. It was driving his

Wolf insane, being so close, and shoved in the corner. Her refusal to acknowledge they were fated to be together was breaking him.

Patience. Be patient. Be worthy of her.

It was difficult, but he had no choice. He needed her. Doubts assailed him whenever he got this bad, and even now he wondered if he could be wrong. Maybe Lucy didn't feel the pull, the bond, not like he did.

No.

That couldn't be true. His Dire Wolf snarled. He was impatient, but he was completely sure Lucy Corwyn was his one and only. Sassy, pigheaded, smart, funny, beautiful, infuriating, perfect, gorgeous, sexy ass woman. Fuck, he loved her.

Feeling it, and admitting it, were two different things, but right then, he had no choice. He loved her, exasperating little tidbit that she was. They had a working garage and a top class mechanic right there, but did she listen? No. She'd insisted on keeping her car at that damn human pervert's garage instead of letting him bring it here. Kept right on ignoring him about everything and anything until he thought he would lose his damn mind.

Furniture moved, and she whimpered softly, but he still heard her. Fuck. She was not going to make it through tonight. He felt it. His animal had been attuned to her every molecule, and it was just getting worse. He'd made some calls, found out about feline Shifters, and knew the hell that was coming for his sweet Lucy.

Feline Shifters experienced a different kind of heat cycle than others. More intense, designed to propagate the species. Sometimes, the pain was so intense, it caused females to accept males they would never look at otherwise. The thought made Derrick furious. He would kill anyone who touched a hair on his mate's head without her consent. Himself included.

I am fucked. So fucked.

The scent of her incoming heat cycle had grown each minute they spent together. As a male Dire Wolf, the closest he would ever come to that was the *mating fever*. It was a compulsion, a biological imperative that would soon take over rational thought and any semblance of reason. Mating fever threatened to consume him, but he was fighting it.

Things were so intense between him and Lucy right now, the rest of the Pack had taken to going out for long rides on their bikes after their shifts, trying to give them space. The rides were hard on them, the open road calling, but every day, they came back. His Pack was trying to settle, but instead of being there for them, he was caught up in his own battle of wills.

His Changes were out of control. Man to beast and back again. He could not go a few hours without shifting into his massive black Dire Wolf, something unheard of for most Shifters. But trying to control his animal, like his emotions, was like trying to keep a tidal wave from hitting the shore.

Please, Lucy, he begged inside his mind's eye.

He saw more than she knew. Understood her reticence was partly because of a childhood she could not control. Trust issues were bound to be a problem, but he could only hope by being steadfast she'd see he was in it for the long haul. She was not getting rid of Derrick. No way, no how.

Stopping his Wolf from taking what the beast already saw as his was hard fucking work. But Derrick was not kidding when he said he would never harm a hair on her head. He would never trick or force her into accepting him. That was not the way he wanted to claim her. No, he wanted her to come to him, ready and willing. Not forced by some side effect of their supernature, she could not even begin to manage.

In his hand, he held something he'd had to search

long and hard for. An elixir, a potion, of sorts, he'd learned about from Thor and his contacts with the Guardians of Chaos. That elite group of Shifter warriors had a calling all their own, but among them was a Witch and scientist who'd developed an agent that could theoretically stop or stifle a female Shifter's heat cycle.

Derrick was uncertain about it, but he trusted Thor. He knew what he had to do, and as he listened to her moving upstairs, her discomfort loud though she tried to be quiet. No more stalling, his Wolf snarled and chomped inside his mind's eye. The huge, prehistoric Wolf's instinct was to be everything his mate needed, and that meant claiming her before her heat began.

No. We will give her the choice.

Derrick heard the stories. If he denied her during her heat, she would suffer immeasurable pain, and there was no way he could do that. Already his feelings echoed with love and complete devotion for his Lucy. Crazy or not, it was just the way he was built. And every inch of him, heart included, was built for her.

His hands clenched tightly at his sides, Derrick was aware of her every move as he stalked her to the bedroom he'd originally claimed as his own. He hoped they could make it theirs together, but he could wait. For her, he would wait forever.

He never expected to be this caught up in her, but it was out of his realm of control. Not something an Alpha could admit easily. The sound of one of the other bedroom doors opening broke his concentration, and he turned to find his cousin waiting, staring at the floor.

"I came to apologize for the uniform and other things this week, you know," Sheila said, and he could tell from her scent she meant it. "I didn't mean nothing by it, Derrick, just thought maybe you needed a little prodding."

"Thank you, Sheila. Unnecessary though. But I don't need any prodding. I know what I want, and I will get there. You don't need to help me, cousin."

"Alright, I guess, I'm just kind of hopeful now that you've found the one. I mean, she's really your mate, right?"

Big green eyes met his for a flash before she averted them in reverence to his position and dominance.

"Yes," he said, and fierce pride filled him with the admission. "She's my mate."

"Then what are you waiting for?"

Derrick thought carefully before speaking, his

eyes riveted to the door that kept Lucy separated from him for the moment.

"She needs time, Sheila. I'm going to do everything I can to give it to her."

"Why don't you go for a run? I can keep watch," Sheila offered.

"That's not a bad idea. Might help me expel some of this energy. Will you give this to her? It's supposed to help with her heat," he murmured, handing the vial to Sheila.

It was probably best if he did not see her right now. Once whiff of her delicious scent, and his animal might wrest control from him. Derrick refused to do that to her. He wanted her so badly, but only when she was ready. Not one second before.

"I will," Sheila said, taking it from him. "You know, you are going to make a wonderful mate."

Outside the Pack house, Derrick growled. He felt on edge and angsty, knowing his mate was inside and about to imbibe a potion to stop something he wanted to revel in. That made him a selfish prick, but he could not help it. He wanted to see her through her heat cycle. To be there to sate her every need and desire. To put a cub inside her belly.

Fuck. He got hard just picturing her swollen with

his young. A little feline that looked just like her would be his choice. Derrick had only seen her Shifted once, and the female had knocked his socks off. She had soft, gold fur and gorgeous violet eyes. So sleek and majestic, powerful though petite. He fucking loved her animal, wished she could run with him tonight.

Tucking away his human skin, Derrick shifted into his midnight black Dire Wolf with hardly any effort. His change was so quick, he moved from skin to fur in the blink of an eye. His pile of clothing rested next to the largest pine in the woods behind their house, and he gazed over at it, checking to make sure all was right. He lifted his lupine head towards the room where Lucy was.

Safe. Inside. Mine.

Turning around, he prepared to run. His Alpha Wolf ready to scout the area, make sure it was secure for his mate and his Pack. It was another one of those Dire Wolf things, an instinct as old as time to care for and protect what was his.

The property they'd bought was bigger than he'd hoped for, with almost five acres' worth of land surrounding them. Putting their mark on all three structures, the house, bar, and garage had settled something in his beast, and over the past few weeks, he and his Pack had roamed these woods and marked the lands that belonged to them, warding off any other predators in the area of the wild and supernatural persuasion.

Security was extremely important to Derrick and his Pack. They'd had run-ins before with other supernaturals who thought taking on a Pack of beasts as powerful as Dire Wolves would give them some sort of up in the paranormal world. The problem was, there were not many who could take on a full grown Dire Wolf and live to talk about it. As he'd gotten older, Derrick had found he'd lost the taste for blood and vengeance. He had nothing to prove to anyone.

His black Wolf took off at a run, leaping over the roots and rocks that littered this part of the forest floor. It was early spring, and though the days were pleasant, the nights were cold. But the wind felt good against his thick, dark fur, and Derrick relished running through it.

His animal refused to stray far from the house, knowing his mate was inside, Even with Sheila's reassurance that she would stand guard, Derrick wasn't comfortable leaving Lucy for long. He imagined it would get worse after he claimed her.

When? Soon. Soon. Soon. Please soon.

Shaking his impatience off, Derrick leaned down to drink the cool, clear water that bubbled from a small brook a few hundred yards behind his house. Lions roamed the other side of his property, but this watering hole was used by both. A neutral ground they'd agreed upon after he'd met with the Blue Valley Pride's own Lion king.

Interesting times, he mused as the refreshing liquid slid down, soothing his beast's throat. The constant growling ever since he'd met Lucy was the reason for the ache there and the water felt good, healing the mild hurt he couldn't help inflicting on himself. But there was only one thing that could soothe the fire inside his blood.

Lucy.

Just thinking her name seemed to conjure that wildly enticing scent of hers as if by magic. He closed his eyes and took a moment to savor the fragrance. His chest rumbled and Derrick felt as if he were being watched. Eyes snapping open, he turned in the direction of something rustling in the brush behind him. Then he came face to face with the cutest damn thing he ever saw.

Lucy's she-Cat slunk forward, bathed in moonlight, her fur glowing in golds and platinum. His lupine eyes memorized her in an instant. From the tips of her pointed ears to her short, powerful legs, cute, stubby tail, and razor-sharp, claw-tipped paws —*she was beautiful.*

The thing he loved most was her eyes. They glowed bright like amethysts in the darkness. He could not believe she was really there, with him, in her fur. Lucy approached with the same air of regality she maintained on two legs, and he chuffed appreciatively as he watched her smooth gait. Purring loudly, she shocked the shit out of him when she rubbed her smaller body along his left flank.

Derrick's Dire Wolf froze. He stood there soaking in the pleasure of her presence while she continued to mark him with her scent. Unsure of what to do next, he waited for her lead. He did not want the meeting to end. So, he remained still and quiet, allowing her animal to sniff and rub and swipe her rough tongue over his snout until she lay before him and closed her eyes. Derrick's Wolfen gaze blazed gold with pleasure at the ease with which her animal half seemed to accept him.

He only wished her human side was as accommodating. Then again, maybe not. There wasn't a thing he would change about her. Lucy was perfect as she was.

Derrick watched her, wondering what he should

do next, wishing she would tell him, but he needn't have bothered. With her next breath, Lucy's form began to twitch and shimmer with that same familiar magic all Shifters used to merge back and forth from fur to skin. Naked and bare in front of him, she waited a beat, purple eyes still glowing before reaching forward and touching her warm hands to his fur.

"You're so big," she whispered. "Much larger than any of the Wolves I've ever seen before."

At that his Wolf growled, and she smiled, a small sound that seemed to shock her as it escaped her lips.

"No need to get jealous. You're much more handsome, too. So strong and soft. So beautiful. I heard you, you know. When you were talking to Sheila."

So that was it, he mused, and allowed her to continue petting and stroking his fur. She'd been listening when his cousin had approached to speak to him.

"Will you turn back for me?"

It was all the invitation he needed. One second, he was his Wolf, the next, he was a man. Fuck, she was stunning, and he could not help himself, he had to touch her.

"Did you get the potion?" he asked, unsure what else to say.

"I did."

"You know, I left to give you space, Lucy. Following me out here is making me think all sorts of things, so tell me now if I have it wrong," he whispered, baring his soul as he ran his fingertips lightly down her forearm. Fuck, she was so soft.

"I got the potion, Derrick. But I didn't take it," she whispered, eyes going to half-mast as he traced the curve of her elbow next.

"Lucy, if you want to wait still—" he tried to warn her, hearing his voice raw and rough with his animal. Fuck, it was barely more than a growl, even to his own ears. Husky and deep, ripe with need, as he took in her luscious body in all its glory.

"It was the most thoughtful thing anyone has ever done for me," she explained, and her eyes swelled with tears. "You tried to help me keep my power. You could have forced the decision, using my heat to stake your claim, but instead you found a way to quell it."

"I didn't mean to overstep, darlin', but I couldn't bear to think of you in pain, he confessed, heart breaking at the sight of her tears.

"You didn't overstep. You did good, Derrick. So fucking good, and I am damn lucky you're mine."

"What are you saying?" he asked, fearing to hope.

"I'm saying I've got no secrets left, Derrick. You've completely surprised me at every turn. When I expect you to act one way, you go and do something else. You've been patient, caring, understanding, and I want—" she paused, stuttering, and wiping her face.

"What do you want, Lucy? I'll give it to you. Anything you want, darlin', it's yours," he vowed.

"I want the impossible. I know you and I are mates, I can feel it, my Cat can too, but I did not want to do this because of my heat cycle. I wanted to make the choice," she said, and he could see the vulnerability clear as day in her violet gaze.

"I gave you the potion, take it, and the choice is yours, Lucy. I know my choice. My Wolf chooses you, and so do I."

"Even if you don't know everything about me?"

"I know all I need to. You're honest and loyal, tenacious too. You don't take handouts, and you've worked for everything you have. You're sassy, badass, and I fucking love your hybrid Cat. You're beautiful, kitten. You are the sexiest woman I have ever seen. Your body, your lips, your hair. And those incredible eyes. They slay me every time," he said, going for broke now.

"I want your eyes to be the first thing I see every morning, the last before I go to bed, and when I am done with this world, I want those eyes to be the last thing I ever see. I am yours for the taking, Lucy. You own me. Looking at you is heaven, but breathing you in, touching your petal soft skin, is pure ecstasy."

"Derrick," she moaned his name.

"Lucy, I'm about half mad to have you. Go now, take the potion, I'll wait. However long it takes. I will wait," he promised.

"What if you get tired of waiting?"

The cool grass felt good against his heated body as he raised her face by her chin. He wanted her to look at him when he said what he had to next.

"I mean it. I will wait as long as you need me to. But know this, I know my own heart, Lucy. I *love* you. I *need* you. I *want* you. Only you. Whatever is going on in that pretty head of yours, understand this. I *know* you, Lucy."

He held her chin when she would've turned her head, firmly yet gently, between his thumb and fore-finger. Truth time.

"I know you've never had a real home. I've got that in common with you. I know you've never had a

Pack or people you can trust. I know you've never trusted a man before, but I swear here and now, in front of the whole damn world, if you take that risk, if you trust me, I will be your home, Lucy."

"Dammit, Derrick," she gasped, but he was relentless. He needed to get this out, needed her to listen.

"If you stay with me, if you have faith in us, I will be everything you need. I'm it, darlin'. I'm your home," he growled.

"That's what I'm afraid of. You'll be my whole world and if you leave, what will I have?" She ducked her head back down, and he wanted to burn her doubts to the ground, kill whoever it was that made her feel this way.

"I can't say I will never hurt you, because I'm bound to fuckup, but I swear it won't ever be intentionally. I will never leave you, Lucy. I couldn't. It would be like cutting off my own leg. We are fated mates. You would know if I was lying. I can't lie to you, kitten. I love you, Lucy. I want to claim you as my mate, take you as my own if and when you will let me. But first, let's get one thing clear, when I say I am your home, you need to understand, you are mine too. And I will always fight for my home."

"Yeah?" Her whispered question stroked his skin like hands ghosting over his soul.

"Yes," he said, and pushed his will into the word, unable to resist trying to make her feel the strength of his vow.

"Alright. Yes."

"What?" He almost couldn't believe what he was hearing, then she smiled.

"I said yes, Derrick. No potions. No more waiting. Yes. My answer is yes."

"Yes?"

"What are you waiting for, Alpha?" She smiled and bit her lip.

Passion and hunger exploded inside of Derrick's blood. He reached out, his Wolf right there with him, as he stroked the rose petal soft skin of her throat and face with trembling hands before lowering his head and crashing his lips to hers.

"Open your mouth," he commanded, dipping inside the hot cavern and penetrating the warmth with his tongue in a mimicry of what his body longed to do.

He eased between her legs, bearing down on her with all his weight, yet careful not to crush her. This was everything good and right with the world. He knew when he'd come here, this place was for him.

Felt it in his bones that he was somehow meant to be there. With the forest floor as their bed, the grass cushioning her body beneath his, Derrick was finally about to make Lucy his. He couldn't have pictured a more perfect landscape for their first time.

Lucy's eyes widened and he could read astonishment and apprehension as his sex came into contact with hers. More than that, she was afraid. He realized, and it dawned on him that his sassy little mate was not used to this kind of intimacy.

Made him wonder what kind of men she'd known before, but he quickly shut the thought down. As far as his Wolf was concerned, she was his period. No one came before and nothing else mattered. Just the two of them. Lucy whimpered, and he made sure she was looking at him before he spoke.

"You think this will be over fast and easy, I see it in your face," he whispered as he dropped kisses along her throat, then looked up to meet her gaze. "You're wrong, kitten. I want you to get used to my weight, to feel how this is going to be. I want your body to know mine before I take you."

"You're so big, Derrick," she said, as if it were a secret. He smiled against her mouth, savoring her precious innocence.

"I promise I will never hurt you like this," he whispered, and he took her mouth with his, kissing her until she softened beneath him.

"You're gonna beg for me before you get me," the huskiness of his voice penetrated the night air.

"Cocky," she whimpered, but already she was unfurling beneath him.

So responsive. So sexy. So mine.

Born from the same desire that had clouded his mind the last few days, sheer delight and tender amusement flowed through him at her innocent whispers and soft hands. Understanding dawned and the prehistoric animal he shared his soul with howled against the night sky. Imagine, under all that sass, his little she-Cat was demure and shy. His Wolf growled deep inside the recesses of his mind, his every Alpha instinct demanding he mark and claim her now. He would wait not one second longer.

Mine.

CHAPTER 9

When Sheila knocked on her bedroom door after Derrick had left, Lucy did not know what to think. She had heard their whole conversation. Knew about the potion he'd procured for her. Her heart had almost trampled her body to death when he'd vowed to give her all the time she needed.

"You did that on purpose?" Lucy asked Sheila.

"Yes, but not to butt in. Derrick is my cousin, Lucy, but he is also the Alpha. What he feels affects us all, and he's been on edge. So, I want to know, are you gonna put him and us out of our misery? Are you gonna let him claim you?"

"Yes," she'd said, knowing full well she was. Sheila handed her the vial and Lucy looked at it in her hands. It seemed so small, but the gesture was huge.

"Yes, I am going to let him claim me. And I am going to claim that big man right back," she proclaimed, and wondered what the hell she was waiting for.

"Lucy!" Sheila had screamed when she opened the second-story bedroom window and vaulted out.

She looked up and laughed at the stunned Dire Wolf female. Sheila looked horrified, but Lucy just laughed.

"Cat's always land on our feet," she chided, then grabbed the hem of her nightgown and tossed it over her head, shifting from skin to fur in an instant.

Seemed forever ago, but it was only minutes. Now, she was here, with him, her almost-mate, in their makeshift forest bed. Lucy's entire body was a shivering mass of nerves. She felt new, untried, and totally at his mercy. But to her utter shock and delight, Lucy trusted him to take care of her.

She couldn't quiet the moans and pants escaping her lips as Derrick pressed his immense body onto hers, crushing her into the soft cool grass with all his delicious weight. Her she-Cat hissed and clawed inside of her, wanting to take part in this mating dance they were beginning. But what did she know about claiming a mate? For the first time in her life, she was trusting herself with someone else. Derrick was kind and good, and hers. All hers. Her instincts demanded she let him steer the way, and once she gave herself over to his control, she knew she'd been right.

"So beautiful," he growled, kissing her with deep, deliberate strokes of his tongue.

There were no half-ways or maybes about it as he plundered her mouth and ran his rough hands over her skin. Lucy couldn't hide behind her sassy mouth here. She had no armor to protect herself, and her all too vulnerable heart was pounding inside her chest like mad.

"That's it, kitten. Touch me," he grunted as her trembling hands slid up his tattooed arms and down his muscular back. Up, down, all the way to his firm ass as his clever mouth sucked on her neck, then down, down, down till he reached the tops of her aching breasts.

"Just like that, darlin'. Drive me crazy with those nails," he groaned, taking her nipple into his mouth.

Lucy raked her claws back up to his shoulders and held his head to her chest as he did unimaginable things to her. Her body tensed and moisture pooled between her legs, she felt her stomach tense as her heat started right then and there. Derrick's mouth was driving her insane. Her body ached and heated, her cycle prompted by sex with her mate, making her ready to receive him.

Derrick's growling never abated as he licked, sucked, and nipped at her tender skin. He was marking her even now, in this small way, making her Cat yowl inside her head. A deep, dark, burning need born of desperation and the absolute certainty he was her mate began to throb throughout every single inch of her body, heart, and soul.

"Mine," he growled, and she nodded.

Every single part of her longed for him, wanted him in new and exciting ways. Frightening ways that would have mortified her had it been anyone else. But this was Derrick. Her mate, who was fated by the universe to be hers and hers alone. *Mine.*

Their sweaty bodies writhed against each other in a dance old as time. Intuition took over, and though her body was on fire for him, her mind was right there with her every step of the way. No more doubts, no more questioning whether this was right. Lucy was very aware of every single thing happening, and she welcomed them.

There was something about acting on impulse and feeling instead of hashing through everything a million times in her head that made her pulse quicken, sweetening every kiss and caress. She wouldn't have to wonder what it felt like to be possessed by this sublime specimen of a man for much longer.

Lucy moaned as his head dipped lower still, licking a trail from her belly button to her thick thighs. This was not like anything she'd ever felt in her limited experience with men. Derrick was not just claiming her body, he was staking claim to her very soul. Gold eyes met hers, his heated breath warming her skin.

The moment was intense, maybe because it was long overdue, but she was glad she'd waited. Glad she'd held onto her heart like it was a precious gift she could only give once. Glad even more that it was his to receive. She only hoped she could satisfy his hunger, sate his need.

"You are all I ever want. Everything I need," he said, and she realized she'd spoken aloud.

Lucy's body beat with a wildly throbbing ache that was scary and yet so damn sweet she wanted to cry. He was powerful and enormous, with hard planes and curved muscles—a creature of pure masculine beauty. She quivered and shook as his lips explored every silken inch of her.

Mouth wide in a soundless moan, she gasped and watched stars explode in the night sky above as Derrick licked his way down her body, eliciting pleasure from nerve endings she had no idea even existed. His shoulders spread her legs wide, and she moaned his name, crying out as she watched him take her sex in a hot kiss that left her begging for more.

Her eyes rolled back as he continued to lap and suckle her plump nether lips, causing moisture to drip down her thighs as he coaxed her body to unimaginable heights. To say she'd never felt this way would be a gross understatement. Lucy was a Shifter, and as such, she was aware of her body in ways no human could ever begin to know.

As his fingers dipped into her sheath, Lucy tensed. Two long, thick digits pushed and pressed inside of her tightness. Their way made easier by the moisture from his tongue and her own body. Tight, tight, tight, and he was big. So big. Even his fingers were large.

"So pretty and pink. Taste so good, kitten. You been saving this for me, haven't you?" he moaned and held her down with one hand when she would've shied away.

"Derrick," she whimpered and gasped, wanting him to finish it, to take her all the way.

"Hold on, love," he growled, and looked at her, his eyes glowing gold with his Wolf.

Lucy nodded, trusting him, she spread her legs wider and watched fascinated when instead of plunging between her folds, he went back to using his tongue and lips to suck her into the most intense pleasure she'd ever felt. On and on, wave after wave of pure, unadulterated bliss blasted through her. Lucy cried out in pleasure, made that much more intense when he slid up her body and pushed his thick, hard shaft into her.

"Mine," growled Derrick.

He moved over her, staying his hips as his thick, beautiful cock pulsed, buried deep inside her. Her gaze found his, fascinated by his intense gold stare. His Wolf was showing, taking part, and yes, she gloried in it.

"Tell me," he demanded, pulling all the way out, leaving her empty, clenching on air. "Say you are mine."

Heat and desire filled her stomach as she looked down to where he stroked himself. Yes, he was denying her his body, but at the same time she was hypnotized by the vision of him touching himself.

His mushroomed head leak a perfect pearl of precum, and Derrick's eyes blazed gold fire.

Her mouth watered. Lucy wanted it, wanted him so badly. She needed him filling her mouth, her pussy, everywhere. Wanted his bite, his claim, now more than ever. Some long forgotten primal instinct was driving her now.

"Tell me," he ordered again, and his voice broke through the haze of her brain.

"Yours. I'm yours. Only yours," she replied.

Derrick grunted, satisfaction in his gaze as he dipped his head and claimed her mouth, and pushed back inside her. Thank. Fuck. She tasted herself on him, and it was wild and erotic, and only when she opened her mouth, and he plunged his tongue inside did he move his hips.

Thank. Fuck.

"Make me yours. Claim me," she begged as her pussy clenched, her next orgasm already starting.

The cocky Wolf grinned wickedly, his eyes glowing and she realized he'd been right. She was begging him. At the moment, Lucy was too far gone to care. Her entire body was on fire. She'd been empty and raw before, and she needed him to fill her, to bite her neck, make his claim, complete their mating.

"Derrick," she growled, thrusting her hips in hopes of enticing him to hurry.

He merely smirked and grunted as he moved his body, switching angles with deep, deliberate strokes. Cupping her face, he made sure to capture her eyes with his own as he kissed her again, tongue pressing into her mouth at the same time his cock moved inside her tight channel.

Magic man. Sex god. Mine. Mine. Mate.

Derrick's smoky, woodsy flavor teased her senses as he coaxed her muscles into relaxing for him, accepting every single bit of his enormous, magnificent cock. He ground his hips, thrusting deeper and deeper into her. Every second that passed brought new waves of arousal, increasing her need and her pleasure.

So much pleasure, almost too much, she thought as she gave control of her body completely over to him.

Derrick seemed to know, seemed to understand what she wanted before she did. He stroked and caressed her, pressing deeper inside of her in one long sliding move till she couldn't tell where he ended and she began. His husky voice seemed all around her in the darkening woods. He whispered naughty phrases of praise and celebration while working them both towards the same goal.

Guided by instinct and the fierce need to claim her mate, Lucy rolled her hips, trying with all her might to pull him deeper, to suck the cum from his body. Her body trembled, blood burned, and heart pounded with need. She wanted it all. Every last drop.

Loosening his hold on her face, his hands roamed down her neck and shoulders to caress her breasts and tweak her nipples as he started moving in earnest. Faster and harder, his deep thrusts became more frantic. The scent of their combined need was thick and potent in the air.

Lucy could hardly breathe as pleasure wrapped around her like manacles, chaining her to him. The imagery just as arousing as the act itself. And she would do it, too. She would willingly place chains around her arms and feet and slide the lock closed herself. Yes, she wanted this mating. Wanted him and the pleasure he brought her, longed to be connected to him, bound to him, mated to him forever.

"Yes," she cried out as the pleasure grew.

The warmth started in her belly, making her feel heavy and hot with the impending explosion that promised to be even better than her first orgasm with him. Claws out she scratched his shoulders, marking her the way felines do as her gums ached with her fangs. She saw the same need, the same instinct, reflected in his gold eyes.

The Wolf was watching her, waiting for the moment their stars aligned. It was the perfect time to seal their mating, a gift the Fates had set in motion eons ago. Blessed, they were both blessed to have found each other. She fully believed that now.

And, suddenly, she was there. Stars exploded behind her eyes as her sex gripped his cock in the most magnificent culmination she'd ever imagined. Derrick roared as his seed coated her womb, he turned her head and bit down, staking his claim where her shoulder met her neck, marking her as his one true mate.

Lucy roared her joy, then she struck in a mirror image of her own mating mark. Lucy bit Derrick, piercing his skin and swallowing his essence with pride. He tensed and squeezed her to him as he spilled even more cum inside of her, triggering another orgasm until the evidence of it was running down her thighs.

Several minutes later, Derrick lapped at her wound, closing the bitemark with his healing saliva. He held her close while she did the same. They were both breathless, boneless, but he still found strength to kiss her head and caress her back as if she were precious, coveted. The thought warmed her as she felt him lift her. She moaned and snuggled, not expecting the cold, as he plunged them into the brook's frigid water.

"What the heck?" she screamed as he sank them both down into the shallow and ice-cold stream.

"Come here, mate," he whispered, smiling as he caught her lips with his own. "Feels good on all that overheated skin, right?"

"Yes, but you could have warned me," she said, smiling back reluctantly, and kissing him to help soothe her shock.

Lucy closed her eyes, allowing him to take all her weight as he tended her and bathed them both in the clear water.

"I didn't know you had a stream," she said.

"You didn't know *we* had a stream," he countered.

"That's right, *we*," she replied and smiled, unable to stop once she started.

He lifted her out of the brook, carried her back to the house, up the staircase to their bedroom. The hallways were empty, and she smiled, knowing that *their* Pack must have heard them in the woods and made themselves scarce. Privacy was a luxury amongst Shifters.

She'd expected Derrick to strut a bit, but in all honesty, he seemed more concerned with caring for her, and that touched her deeply.

Good mate. Strong. Loving. Fierce.

"Derrick?"

"Hmm?"

He settled her on the bed after they'd showered in the bathroom with actual soap and water. Her mate had been so lovingly gentle, kissing her silly and patting her skin dry. Her heart squeezed and warmed, and looking at him, she felt like she'd won the damn lottery.

"Are you happy?"

"Are you kidding? You made me the happiest man in the world."

"You still want me after that. No regrets?" she asked, biting her lip. Derrick grinned and took her hand, placing it on his dick. He was long and hard and pulsed beneath her hand.

"Feel this? This happens whenever I am near you. Fuck yes, I want you."

"I'm glad. I want you too," she confessed before straddling his waist.

"Fuuck," Derrick grunted as Lucy kissed his neck, running her tongue over the mark she placed there.

She lifted her hips, placing his head at her ready

entrance, and lowered herself on him. They moaned in unison as she rode him. Derrick was sweet and patient with her fumbling.

"So sexy," he growled, squeezing her breasts with his big hands, and licking every inch of skin he could reach. Lucy could hardly keep up, and finally, she allowed him to guide her into a rhythm that satisfied them both.

"More, I want more," he growled, and lifted her, flipping her over onto her hands and knees.

Her inner kitty went wild, yowling as he stroked her cheeks, slapping one hand down on her ass as he found her with his cock, filling her with one hard thrust. This was the claiming her animal wanted, *no*, demanded. She pushed back instinctively. Hissing, she looked over her shoulder and saw his Wolf glowing gold in his eyes.

"Take me hard, Derrick."

"Mine," he growled, and did just that.

Her mate had more moves than she could have guessed, and he rocked her world with them. With his clever fingers thrumming over her clit and his long, girthy cock filling her so good, it did not take long before she was screaming his name. Then they were both coming. And Lucy felt their bond strengthen even more before he turned her over and kissed her slowly and carefully.

Sweet, tender mate.

"Derrick?"

"Yeah, love?"

"I love you, *mate*," she said before sleep took her.

CHAPTER 10

The next few days were like something out of a dream. Derrick's Wolf had stopped pacing and growling. He watched Lucy all the time, wondering at the hole she'd filled inside him. His mate was so beautiful and tough, the perfect combination of sweet and sassy. She fit in with his Pack, with him, and he was just so damn proud to call her his.

Right now, she was laughing at something Cole said, but he was not paying any mind to their words. He was too stuck by her beauty. Her hair was shiny and thick, long like he liked it. He imagined it as it had been that very morning, spilling across his pillow like a bolt of silk.

He'd had those tresses wrapped around his hand

when she'd surprised him with a morning BJ. In his wildest dreams, Derrick had never imagined he'd be waking up to find his cock buried deep in Lucy's succulent mouth.

"I guess cats really like cream," he'd mused aloud, and winced at the slap she'd given him right on his ass after that remark.

They'd had a spank war then, and just thinking of his pink handprint on her luscious, rounded ass made him hard. Oh yeah, his little hellion was definitely into spanking. Something they'd be exploring together in the near future.

Grrr.

"When are you gonna let me bring your car over here, Luce? You know Big Tom isn't gonna take care of it like I would," Cole stated.

"Well, he already started the repairs. I feel bad about taking the work from him," his surprisingly tenderhearted mate returned.

True, he'd tried several times to get her to allow him to bring the old Ford here for Cole to fix, but she wouldn't hear of it. His sassy little mate insisted she pay for it too. Damn stubborn woman.

Isn't she great?

He noted the dark pink blush that swept up her face when he caught her gaze, and his heart damn near stopped beating inside his chest. So pretty. Beautiful with milky white skin and crazy gorgeous purple eyes. They reminded him of wild bull thistles, the kind he passed a million times on the open road.

He'd seen his share of wonders in the world, but looking at her was better than any ocean shore, desert sunset, or mountain view. Yeah, he'd missed the open road, but this was home now, in more ways than one. Lucy bit her lower lip before flashing him a smile, the one that drove him wild, and he felt his body respond instantly.

He loved her sweet innocence, headstrong retorts, and responsive nature. He'd worried his hunger for her would scare her, but not his mate. Her appetites were as insatiable as his. Lucy was a firecracker in bed. Fantastic in and out of it. Her desire was more than a match for his own, as was her heart.

His mate's loving nature was so big, she could more than take her place at his side. Lucy might be a tiny little feline hybrid, but she was the undoubted Alpha fem of their Dire Wolf Pack. Caring for each of them in her own way. Getting them total, and joke when they'd been worried and nervous about settling. She was a tonic for them all.

"Hey there, kitten," Derrick called as he walked over with a cold bottle of sweet tea in his hand.

"That for me?"

"Yes, ma'am," he drawled, and held the bottle to her lips.

Hunger flared to life as he watched her small, pink tongue lick a drop of the brown liquid from the rim.

"Okay, you two, I'm out," Cole muttered, and the smart Wolf walked away.

"Missed you," Derrick said, pressing her against the wall of the garage, and lifting her in his arms until he could comfortably settle between her denim-clad legs.

"Hmm, did you?" She smiled and mashed her mouth to his.

"Yeah. I fell back asleep, and you left. I don't like waking up without you," he said.

"Sorry, I, uh, had an appointment," she replied, and he frowned.

He'd been getting used to waking up with his arms full of his mate's luscious curves. Today he'd missed that. Only the note she'd left on the pillow stopped him from losing his mind and taking off after her. As it was, he'd still called her cell.

"What was the appointment for?" he asked with

mild interest as he nibbled that sweet spot under her chin where her neck met her chest.

"You know that shop in town where Sheila got my, *uh*, uniform?"

Lucy sighed and tilted her head back to give him better access as his tongue traced the line of her ample cleavage. His Wolf had developed quite the appetite for her berry-pink tipped delights. He wanted them again. Now.

Grrr.

"Yeah, what about that shop?" he inquired, as he tugged the neckline down and lifted one sweet mound out for his lips to catch and suckle.

"Oh gods," she moaned, but continued to talk.

It was a little game they played. To see how long either could go with a conversation before they lost their minds in each other's bodies.

"I, uh, had to order a few more things," she hedged, biting her lower lip and pulling on his hair to get him closer.

He laughed and bit down gently, loving the way her smile peeked out at him. Derrick frowned then as her words filtered in through his lusty haze, and he pulled free of her glorious breast.

"What things?"

"Oh, well, I needed some tops in larger sizes."

"What for? I told you, kitten, you look gorgeous in everything," he said, and kissed her lips again just because.

"I know. There is a reason, though."

"Such as?"

"This," she said, and tilted her head. "Breathe here," she commanded gently, and pushed his head down against her neck.

Derrick went willingly. God, he loved that part of her. Her mate mark had healed already, but the pink scar was visible. He'd been a little rougher than he'd meant to be, and the resulting mark was rather large.

He ran his nose over it and breathed deep, loving the mingled essence of both their scents that now made up her fragrance. There was something new there, something different. Alarms sounded inside his brain, and he stiffened. Derrick pressed his nose against her neck, eliciting a giggle as he sniffed her skin deeply.

Could it be? Holy. Shit. YES! Warmth and pride filled him at the revelation.

"Lucy, for real? Are you sure? Already?"

He held her closer, eyes wide with wonder. Tears welled in her violet eyes as she placed her hand over his and brought it to her soft lower belly.

"Are you angry?" she asked, and he realized he still had not spoken.

"Angry? Oh my gods, darlin', no, of course not. You have no idea the gift you are," he told her. "A baby. Our baby. Fuck, I love you," he whispered, breaking down a little.

He let her see his emotions overflow for a moment before he kissed her again. Softer, slower this time, with his hand pressing the button that would shut the garage door, closing them in and away from the rest of the world.

It took less than a second before he lost control and crushed himself to her front. His claws sliced through her clothing until she straddled him as he leaned back on the seat of one of the classic Harleys he'd bought to work on before she'd arrived in his life.

"I've been wanting you to take me for a ride on one of your bikes," she moaned as he lavished attention on both her breasts while one hand spread her dripping slit and he found her hidden bundle of nerves.

"How about you ride me instead," he groaned as he freed himself from his jeans and entered her in one hard thrust.

Derrick could not seem to get enough of his

mate's amazing body. He never would either. With this news, he needed to be inside her, to show her the depth of his feelings. Violet eyes wide and glowing with her Cat, Lucy moaned as she rocked her body, taking him deeper and deeper. Hands gripping the plump globes of her sexy as fuck ass, he lifted and dropped her hard onto his engorged sex. Fuck, he needed her, wanted her all the time.

"Oh fuck, kitten, you feel so good. Like a velvet vise wrapped around my dick, squeezing me so fucking tight," he growled as he took her mouth and rode the wave of overwhelming pleasure until they were both roaring with it.

Her wicked sharp claws scratched at his skin and his Wolf howled with joy. He loved wearing her marks. Pride and possession flowed through him as her pussy gripped his cock, milking him of his cum.

"Mine," he growled, sucking the skin over her mating mark, causing another series of mini orgasms to rack her sweet body.

Cradling her close, he kissed her head, her eyelids, and every bit of her that he could reach as he lifted her, and himself, off the bike and carried her to the back door. He grabbed a clean drop cloth and placed it over her body before taking her across the yard to the house.

"Oh damn, my eyes," growled his Beta, Brock, who had just dropped the carton of milk he was holding to cover his eyes with both hands.

Lucy giggled from underneath the drop cloth and Derrick growled. After all, it was his ass on display for Brock, Cole, and Thor, who were all sitting in the kitchen. Brock was groaning like an idiot, but the other two simply kept their heads down.

Smart asses.

"Hey Lucy, how ya doin'? Congratulations are in order, then?" Cole asked.

Derrick growled again but stopped once Thor smacked the younger Wolf in the head. At least someone was smarter than they looked, he thought grimly. After a warm bath, he settled his mate in bed and ordered her to take a nap. Not that she listened, but after spending a little time on his knees, enjoying a bit of his favorite snack, he finally wore her out enough to send her to sleep.

Cubs. My cubs. Imagine that?

He dropped a kiss on her brow before heading downstairs. It was Friday night, their busiest night of the week, and he wanted to make sure everything was ready.

"Fucking Weylin. You hide my gauges again?"

Thor growled, lifting the younger Wolf off the floor by the neck.

By the time Derrick walked into the sprawling living room, Weylin's face was the same ruddy shade as his hair. He smacked against Thor's grip, shaking his head and blinking rapidly before the much bigger man let go.

"Fuck, Thor. No! I learned my lesson last time," Weylin gasped and choked.

Derrick walked over to the bookshelf and held up an empty whiskey glass in Thor's direction. He shook it and waited for the beast to drop the younger Wolf.

"Looking for these?"

"Oh, yeah. Thanks, Alpha," Thor grumbled, and took the glass with his Australian Bloodstone plugs.

The giant, bald Enforcer sat down and began the process of cleaning then inserting them into his lobes, not even looking at Weylin who was gasping, face still pink from lack of oxygen.

Derrick had plenty of tattoos, but few piercings. In fact, he'd largely neglected his body art for a while. It was time to begin the process once more, and he waited until Thor was finished before approaching him with the subject. By then, all of his

Pack was there, either standing or sitting in the living room.

They'd been seven for so long, and he was about to change that. It was tough for their kind, living longer and predominantly solitary lives, cut off from normals and other Shifters alike. But Derrick was shaking things up. Setting them up in territory of their own. Claiming a mate. He was making waves—for the better, he hoped.

Yes, it truly was with the best intentions. He wanted to move forward for the good of them all, but most especially, and selfishly, for his own good. Lucy was his salvation, his reason, his everything. Finding a mate, getting her with cubs, was like a dream come true, and he was humbled that she'd chosen him as well. Just as he was humbled when they'd picked him to lead.

Mine, growled the Wolf inside him.

The Pack. Lucy. His babe. All his. Imagine a prehistoric beast like his Wolf completely devoted to his Pack and female. The tiny little she-Cat sleeping upstairs held his heart in his hands even as she carried their cubs beneath hers.

Cubs? He wondered why he was referring to her pregnancy in multiples, but the Wolf inside him merely grinned.

Cubs, the animal responded knowingly.

The atmosphere seemed to sizzle and crack with anticipation. Each of his Wolves knew about his mating, and yet they'd been waiting for him to make the official announcement. This was the way of his kind. A sacred culmination of events that had begun eons before he was even an idea. It was time to seal the mating bond.

"Well, you gonna spit it out or what?" Sheila asked, breaking the tension as she usually did.

"Sheila," grumbled Brock.

"We all heard you two in the woods the other night, and if we were dumb enough to miss that, we've been hearing it in here the last few days. I'm really glad we went with the soundproof insulation," Phoenix added.

"You gonna tell us or what?" Sheila prompted, grinning wider.

"Tell us what?" Weylin asked, grunting when Thor thumped him on the head yet again.

"You all know Lucy is my mate. Yes, I have given her my mark, and she's given me hers," he waited a beat for the ruckus to die down before continuing.

All the whooping and congratulations they showered on him felt good and right. Derrick looked each one of them in the eye before speaking, so they knew he was focused on them as their Alpha should be.

"You know, we've been searching for a place to settle, and you also know I chose this spot on nothing more than a gut feeling. I am proud to say Blue Valley is the official home of the Dire Wolf Pack and MC. Now, I have to do something else. Thor, it's time," Derrick said, and looked over at the Enforcer.

Thor was a man of few words, but the deep pride on his face made Derrick glad inside. Pack emotions were channeled through their bonds, and theirs was such it was built on friendship and trust, maybe even more than the usual Shifter dominance hierarchy.

Derrick stood up and stripped his shirt off. It was past time he did this. Adrenaline pumped through him as Brock moved the coffee table, and Thor gathered his things. His Pack gathered around him, and Derrick's chest felt tight with feelings.

Arms clasped, the Dire Wolves formed a circle around Derrick and the big, bald man. They nodded as one and Derrick, the Alpha, dropped to his knees in the middle of them. This was a show of trust, of devotion, of their dedication to each other. Alphas did not go to their knees for anyone.

Thor chanted quietly in an old, forgotten tongue.

He removed a jar from a small metal chest with the ancient glyphs of the original Dire Wolf Pack engraved on it, a sacred relic from their past. Inside was a special ink, magicked by friends of the Dire Wolves to use on their otherwise *tough to penetrate* skin.

This was an old custom. A rite of passage every mated Dire Wolf throughout the ages had gone through. Especially the Wolves who wore their patch. To them, DWMC meant history. It meant brotherhood. It meant a bone deep devotion to one another that no other Pack in existence could claim.

They were descendants of the original wanderers and had lived nomadic lifestyles for generations together. Always together. Occasionally, their Pack broke off into smaller MCs, as Derrick and these six had—but they were still DWMC.

That was who they would always be at their core. That meant loyalty to Pack and family, and in this moment, he was telling his Pack, *his MC*, that Lucy was his family. With this ink, he named her as his true home, just like he told her when he'd claimed her as his mate.

Thor closed his eyes, repeating the sacred prayer in the old language. He then took a long, thin bamboo needle and dipped it into the bottle of ink that never dried or ran out. With smooth efficient moves, he sliced Derrick's skin with the sharpened wood and imprinted the symbol and words of his commitment to Lucy as the Fates willed it through the large male's fingers.

"What's going on?" Lucy's voice reached him from the stairs. His Wolf tensed as he scented her fear and anxiety, but Derrick remained still.

"It's alright, Lucy," Sheila said, and he made a note to thank his cousin as she gestured to Lucy to join their circle at her side.

He followed her movements through the room with his ears. His mate, *his pregnant mate*, stood between Brock and Sheila now. He inhaled her sweet scent, made sweeter now that he could pinpoint the subtle notes of the cubs she carried. He wondered if she was aware she was having multiples yet and allowed a small smile to settle on his face as he thought of her and their young.

"It's almost over," Sheila told Lucy.

"What is he doing?"

"Dire Wolves' tattoos tell our story. The story of our Pack and MC. Our backs are left bare until we find our fated mates. I'm sure my cousin has informed you that you are his, sweet Lucy. This is our way of marking the occasion and recording it for all to witness."

He heard Lucy's intake of breath and noted again the subtle change in her scent. Anxiety and fear became gratitude and, yes, there it was. His favorite scent of all. The scent of her love.

Hope rose in him, as did his love for the woman he'd claimed as his own. He would make sure she knew how he felt every day of their lives together.

Mine.

He was so focused on her he barely felt the pain of Thor's movements as he cut through his tough skin again and again. The smell of his own blood was thick in the air. The wet, warm towel Thor used to wipe away the gore felt good as he worked. Some several minutes later, Derrick felt the bamboo needle stop.

With a grunt and a great intake of breath, Thor sank down onto the floor. As one, the dire Wolf Pack bowed their heads and said their own private thanks to the gods and the Fates alike.

Thor was what the old graybeards of the original DWMC called *favored by the gods,* meaning they sometimes spoke through him. Visions and messages were only part of his special talents. He was also the only one of them to be *touched by the Fates.*

The ritual of the claiming tattoo was sacred among the DWMC. Derrick gave thanks to the Fates for his friend and Enforcer. Thor's gifts went far beyond being the biggest and baddest amongst them, but sometimes they took a lot out of him.

"Thank you, brother," Derrick said, standing up and meeting his Enforcer's gaze, "If you need the night off, take it. We will handle it."

Thor blinked, too drained to do more than that, and Derrick squeezed his shoulder and pressed his forehead to his. A gesture of affection and a way to let him know he was Derrick's to keep safe. As Alpha, it was his duty and privilege. He turned to his mate as Cole ran to the kitchen to bring water and tea for the man who'd just performed the ritual that sealed his claim for life.

"Lucy?" Derrick found her standing on the bottom stair.

"Hey," she said, wiping tears. She touched his shoulders gingerly.

"Turn around," she ordered, once more reminding him she was a sassy little thing.

"Why the tears?" he asked as he turned to show her his mating tattoo.

"Oh, Derrick, it's beautiful, and it's already healing," she exclaimed.

"Tell me what you see," he whispered. He had yet to see the image, only felt its path as Thor carved it across his back and shoulders.

"Your Dire Wolf is laying down on the forest floor, body bent in a semi-circle like around a, a—" She gasped, and he knew she was crying, the need to comfort warred with the need to hear what she had to say.

"Don't turn yet," she told him. "You're lying with your body tucked around a she-Cat. It's me," her voice trembled.

"That's good. My Wolf is protecting you," Derrick answered.

"There's more," she said, and this time he felt her wonder. "Three cubs are playing between us two Wolves, one red and one black, and one she-Cat. She's got one of her brother's tails in her claws." Lucy laughed, and Derrick grinned, picturing it already.

"There's writing, but I can't read it," she told him, as he turned to her.

"Those are Dire Wolf glyphs. Show me what they look like?"

"One is kind of like a circle, but there are two lines twirled around each other inside—"

"That is the symbol for fated mates."

Derrick touched her face hesitantly. Her tears left tracks down her face, and he bent forward to kiss them away.

"I love you, Lucy," he said, and felt his Wolf rise when she pressed her lips so sweetly to his.

"I love you too." She sighed against him, and he wrapped her up in his arms. The new tattoo stretched his skin a bit, but he'd be fully healed in another hour. Thor would've cut deeply to make the ink last.

"Sheila said you're only allowed to have this done once in your life."

"Yes. Unless Fate blesses a Shifter twice with his or her perfect mate, but once is all I need, kitten."

"Yeah?"

"Yeah. You are it for me, love," he said, and his voice dropped to a husky whisper as her violet eyes blinked away a fresh wave of tears.

"Derrick," she whispered and kissed his lips again with all the sweetness and heat she had bubbling up to the surface. "I love you so much."

"I love you back, darlin."

Derrick tugged her closer to him, fierce yet tender. In a short time, this woman had become his entire world. Now everyone would know it.

"You two about done?" Sheila asked, breaking the moment.

"What time is it?"

Lucy asked and looked around for the wall clock. Derrick stopped, finally noticing her outfit.

"Hey? What's this?" he asked and nodded to her short shorts and tank top.

"It's my uniform, Derrick," she explained slowly, like he was an idiot.

"I know that, but why are you wearing it?"

"Because we open in an hour. Did that ink hurt your brain or something?"

"You're not working tonight," he said, and realized his mistake the instant her eyes glittered at him like amethysts.

"Lucy, I mean, um, well, you're carrying our cubs—"

"Don't you call them pups?" she interrupted, and he shook his head, grinning.

So little was common knowledge about his kind. But that was okay. He'd teach her everything she needed to know. Besides, according to the image Thor had seen and tattooed on his back, they would have two Wolves and one she-Cat. Gratitude filled him, followed by a serious wave of protective instinct.

"Actually, we call our young cubs like cats do," he said and nuzzled her neck with his nose and dropped a kiss there.

"Mm, that's nice," she replied and nodded. "Come on, let's go to work."

"Kitten," he said, trying a different tactic. "Don't you think you need to sit this one out?"

"Derrick, I'm like five minutes pregnant. This is going to go on for another six months at least, and I will not sit around like a damn cantaloupe waiting to ripen."

"I think you're perfect, kitten. Let's go to bed," he growled and nipped her ear, wondering if he could maybe entice her to stay home.

"Listen up, Fido, I may like that tongue of yours, but if you want to get it near my body again, you will not try to tell me what to do. Got it? Now, I'm not an idiot, I am not going to risk hurting myself or my cubs for anything. We're just going to the bar."

"I know, but I worry—"

"Derrick, I'm a Shifter," she said, ignoring the snickered *more like a house cat* comment from Sheila. She tossed her blonde hair back and flipped the younger woman the bird, while not taking her eyes off her mate.

"We're still looking for more staff, plus I need

money to pay for my car. Now, are you gonna stand there with your mouth hanging open, mate? Or are you gonna shake that ass and come with me?"

"Damn, Derrick! You are one lucky Alpha. That is one sassy as hell mate you got there," Brock said, grinning at Lucy in a way that set Derrick's teeth on edge.

A sharp elbow to his stomach had Brock bent over and gasping for air before he understood the undercurrents. His eyes widened as he hightailed it out of the house. Just in time, too.

"Sorry, uh, excuse me Alpha, Alpha fem," the man said, burning rubber to get outside.

Derrick couldn't stop his rumbling growl, but Lucy just rolled her pretty purple eyes, turned her back, presenting him with a perfect view of her delectable ass in those soon to be torn up and thrown out cutoffs. Then she stomped out the door.

Fuck, Shit. Grrr.

CHAPTER 11

Serious Moonlight was at full capacity by ten o-clock and Lucy's feet were killing her. Perhaps Derrick was right, and she should have stayed home. Not that she would tell her overprotective mate that. No need to inflate that big head of his. Besides, she could finish out the night.

A full moon hung low in the sky outside, and the place was overloaded with Shifters who were feeling the power that came with the change in the lunar phase. Without Thor there to wrangle the customers, who were a bit enthusiastic, the job had been mostly left up to Derrick.

She watched him when she could and there was no doubt about it, her Alpha was one tough mutt. Still, something was off. She'd been on edge all night. Her thoughts kept drifting to Derrick and his amazing new ink. She took a pic of it with her phone and held it up to him so he could read the glyphs to her.

"It says, 'For each Wolf there is a perfect mate, the road was long and lonely, but the destination complete. Lucy is for Derrick, and he is for her, their hearts forever entwined, a home for each other, united until all the stars burn up in the sky', Then this here is the symbol of my house. Rand literally means 'wolf shield', see that there? There's a feline paw print inside of it now. It means I'm your shield, kitten. I'll protect you and our cubs from the whole damn world."

His words had turned into moans as their mouths crashed together in a long, drawn out kiss Phoenix had interrupted with a fake sneeze. *Idiot,* she smirked and shook her head. The entire Pack was a lot more easy-going than she would have expected of a bunch of tough bikers, who happened to also be giant, prehistoric Wolves.

"Can I get a drink here?"

Lucy turned and faced the same angry customer who'd been tossed out her first night on the job. She stared the man down, but there wasn't much she could do by herself.

"I said, I want a beer. I'm a paying customer," the sour-faced man grumbled.

She couldn't ignore him any longer, but she was uneasy. He should have known better than to come back. There was not much she could do now. Everyone was busy and she could not catch Derrick's eye.

"Okay. One beer, then you need to leave," she told him as she slid a domestic bottle across the bar and took his five-dollar bill.

"I'll leave when I'm ready," he mumbled under his breath, but Lucy still heard him.

She needed to find Derrick, but a group of young human women snagged her attention next, and she spent the next fifteen minutes mixing a bunch of Cosmos. Her thoughts drifted back to the tattoo ritual and Thor. Derrick had explained a little about his gifts. That Shifter certainly had a mystical way about him, despite being enormous, tattooed, and pierced. Or maybe even because of it.

Lucy happened to like the Pack's propensity for ink. She'd have to ask Derrick about acquiring some of her own. That was the thing about Shifters. They tended to heal quickly, and tattoos faded away a lot quicker than they did on humans, but he'd also explained about the special ink they had.

The sound of glass breaking brought her head up, and she watched Weylin vault over the front bar, broom, and dustpan in hand. He efficiently cleared the mess while Derrick made his way from the front door, a concerned expression on his face. Weylin gestured to the slinky blonde woman who'd made the mess and made quick work of the clean-up. Derrick walked the woman around the spill to the bar and got her another drink.

The woman was already tipsy and did not seem to understand what *no* meant. She kept running her hands up his shoulders while he efficiently removed them and frowned when she reached for him again. The woman giggled and tried tugging him back to her side when he replaced her drink, and Lucy growled. Her mate's golden stare found hers, and she closed her eyes for a second. Her feline was turning into a seriously possessive bitch.

She sighed and opened them to find him staring, the female customer happily attached herself to another male, and all was right in the world. He cocked his head to the side, and after a minute, Lucy was surrounded by her mate's wonderful embrace.

"Kitten, you need to stop flashing those gorgeous

eyes of yours at me if you want to keep working," he growled, and dropped a warm, quick kiss on her mouth before turning to fill an order.

"Yes, Alpha," she said and nudged him with her hip.

"Need help back here?" he asked softly, and she felt their bond pulse and beat in time with her heart.

Damn, she'd missed him. Craved his touch, His scent. It was silly. They'd only been right here. Separated by a few measly feet, working for just a few hours. Derrick Rand had officially turned her into some clingy, mated female. Eeek! But she would not have it any other way, she thought as he touched her hip to reach past her for a bottle of booze.

"Are you finished with the door?"

"Brock's on it."

"Then, yes, please. Stay and help me," she replied, loving the smile that lit up his handsome face as he nodded.

Derrick hadn't wanted her to come in tonight, but that was him being protective. Besides, she was glad she did. She enjoyed working beside him. The band tonight was all female, a group of Fox Shifters from Philadelphia calling themselves the *Stealth Vixens*. They were good. Loud, but good.

She liked their country rock rhythm. Brock had

closed the kitchen early, and had taken over as Bouncer for Derrick, so the Alpha could join her at the back bar. He'd spent the last few days working alongside her, and she loved it. Lucy decided then that she was going to work as long as she could fit behind the bar. If Derrick wanted to work beside her, she'd welcome it, but that was up to him.

She had a car to pay for. Not that she needed it for anything since she wasn't leaving her mate obviously, but still. It was hers. She and Buddy—*that was what she called her car*—had been through a lot together. She tried to be angry at Derrick when he unceremoniously bent down and retrieved a case of beer faster than she could, restocking the rear coolers, but she just couldn't.

Really, she wanted to yell at him, to stand up for feminism, but he was just so darn sexy. And that Alpha male attitude of his kind of turned her on. Okay. It seriously turned her on. How had she gone from being nothing but a vagabond, to being claimed and mated to the sexiest damn man, and one of the most powerful Shifters she'd ever met, all in a week's time?

Maybe Fate had finally thrown her a bone, or Karma had finally caught up with her. After being on the road alone for most of her adult life and, if she were interested in looking back, most of her youth, Lucy had finally found a home.

In him.

"You alright?" Derrick asked.

"I love you," she said, feeling the words to her marrow.

"Love you too, mate," he said back, no hesitations.

His warm hands cupped her face and neck, and he dragged his lips across hers in a kiss that screamed of possession. Her stomach tightened and pulse raced. She felt her heart explode with emotion. Lucy could have spent all night kissing him.

She was still lost in his touch when the first scream broke out.

———

Derrick's Wolf snarled and snapped to attention just as all hell broke loose., He shoved his mate gently behind him as not one, but five men, wearing masks, came busting through the doors waving actual fucking torches and screaming profanities.

"What the fuck is going on?" Sheila asked, running over to them from the back room where she'd been getting some bottles to restock the front bar.

"Lucy, stay down! Sheila, protect her!" he ordered.

"I'm fine, Derrick. Go," his mate said, anger and worry making her scent sharp.

"I can't see anything," Lucy said to Sheila, who was already grabbing her hand and pulling her to safety.

"Sheila's got you, Lucy."

"I'm fine, Derrick. Go, get everyone out—"

Smoke billowed, stinging his eyes, and making it difficult to see. Forget about hearing anything. The crowd had begun to stampede at the first sign of trouble. He pushed back against the throng, trying his best to reach the first masked male who was holding what he realized wasn't an old-fashioned torch, but rather was some kind of a homemade holder for a smoke bomb.

"Motherfucker," he roared.

Derrick punched the guy in the face, knocking him out cold, and grabbed the device, ripping it from the hands of the stupid human fuck who thought this would be a good idea.

Another approached, but the fucker went down fast. Weylin ran to him, covering his mouth to stop from choking. He grabbed the torch and took off for the side door with it fast as his Shifter legs would take him. Derrick had another offender by the throat as Brock handled one by the front door. He didn't see the other man until the bastard was on him with a blade of some sort.

"You filthy animals. I know what you are. Get out of our town!" He screamed and slashed at Derrick's forearm.

The fucker cut him, and Derrick's rage boiled as he scented his blood on the air.

"You shouldn't have done that," he growled, dropping the man he'd been holding hard on the ground.

That dick would just have to wait. Derrick turned and faced the man with the huge hunting knife. The human swallowed, the stink of fear and liquor coming off him in waves. This was the same asshole from their opening night. The one whose name he'd given to the Council. Derrick frowned, they should have caught up with him by now.

"Come on, then. You're nothing but an animal. You belong on my wall," he sneered, and Derrick's Wolf pushed forward.

"Oh, I wouldn't do that," the stranger gestured

behind him, and Derrick saw another guy with a video camera pointed at him.

"I'll expose all of you for what you are," the asshole sneered. "And I'll hurt your bitch too."

Derrick turned to see his worst nightmares come true. One of the assholes resurfaced holding some kind of homemade pipe bomb in his hand, and he had Lucy. Sheila was crumpled on the floor, bleeding from her head and Lucy's hands were covering her stomach. Her wide purple eyes met his, and he realized she wasn't afraid. She was waiting. For him.

"That was your last mistake," Derrick growled.

He watched the stupid fucker laugh right before Derrick jumped on him. In an instant, Derrick's Wolf lent him fangs and claws without needing to swap skins. He heard scuffling behind him, recognizing Sheila's snarl as she whooped the would be Spielberg's ass.

Fuck these assholes, he growled and squeezed the man's throat snapping his neck like a twig. Lucy was holding the wrested pipe bomb in her hand and Derrick ran to her, taking it gingerly before running to the door and tossing it hard as he could away from everyone. The explosion was loud and sharp, but small. Still, the entire bar went quiet.

Everyone had started clearing out the moment

chaos erupted, and only a handful of people, Shifters, had remained to round up the bad guys. Eight in all, two dead in the struggle, the other six subdued and waiting for authorities.

The video camera had been wiped and destroyed, no evidence of the Shifter secret would remain for police to discover. Derrick sat on a stool with his arms wrapped around his mate while the investigators finished working the scene. He could have lost her tonight, but his mate had remained levelheaded and calm. She'd trusted him to protect her, and he did his best, but his fierce little she-Cat had really saved herself.

She's safe. Safe. Mine. Protect.

"So, what can you tell us?" asked the lead detective, a Lion Shifter, named Leonard Crowley. Derrick and Lucy went over the incidents again, and the detective took notes.

"We won't be pressing any charges against any of you, as it seems these guys were unhinged and looking for trouble," Crowley said. "The bomb was real. Unfortunately, crimes like this happen from time to time. We got an email earlier and some anti-government organization claimed responsibility for the attack."

"And Derrick won't be charged, you're sure?" Lucy asked.

"No ma'am. He was acting purely in self-defense. He's a hero. Had that bomb gone off, dozens of people would have died."

"Thank goodness," she said, and slumped against him.

"Detective, my girl is tired. I'd like to take her home. If you have any other questions, you can talk to my staff or wait to get in touch with me."

"Will do. Thank you."

"Oh, when can we reopen?"

"Soon as we're done. Shouldn't take more than a few hours," he nodded and walked away.

"Come on, kitten," Derrick rumbled, and scooped Lucy up in his arms.

"You don't have to carry me," Lucy said as she lay her head against his shoulder.

It was just like her to deny she was dead on her feet. He smiled his response and kissed her hair, holding her even closer as he walked them home.

"I saw him sitting at the bar earlier. The guy we threw out on opening night. I am so sorry, Derrick. This is my fault. I just forgot when you came over. I should have told you. I am so sorry," she repeated, and he hated that she blamed herself.

"Lucy, look at me. There was nothing you could have done to stop that lunatic. None of this is your fault and look what you did. You kicked his ass, broke the camera, saved us all from exposure."

"You're not mad?"

"At you? No fucking way. You are a total badass. I am proud of you."

"I just feel responsible—"

"You're not," he insisted.

"Is your arm okay?" she asked softly.

"All healed, kitten," he said, and bent so she could turn the knob on the front door.

Thor stumbled into the kitchen from his room, and Derrick could tell the man was still out of it.

"Something happen?"

"Don't worry about it, brother. We're fine."

"You sure?" he asked, voice hoarse.

"Yeah. Go on back to bed," Derrick commanded.

The big man nodded, and Derrick took the stairs two at a time, taking them straight to the shower. He wanted to wash away the smoke, blood, and the stink of fear at seeing that man holding a bomb on his mate.

"Hey, I'm alright," Lucy said, and stepped under the spray of warm water with him.

She wrapped her arms tightly around him and he

felt himself tremble. Fuck. He could have lost her tonight. It was unthinkable.

"I'm alright, you protected me, your Wolf protected me. My mate, my good mate," she said, dropping kisses across his chest and shoulders until she reached up with small hands and tugged his face down to hers.

———

Lucy could not believe everything that had happened over the last few hours. Her strong, protective, amazing mate had taken down a bunch of lunatics who'd wanted to cause real harm to them. Humans were not supposed to know about Shifters, but that angry customer sure seemed to know too much. It was a huge problem, and she hoped the Council acted this time instead of sitting on their hands.

But none of that mattered right now. The only thing that concerned her was getting her big, sexy mate to reaffirm their connection. After their warm shower, where Derrick had insisted on washing her body from head to toe, he'd wrapped her up in a fluffy towel and carried her to the bed.

"Lucy, I need you. Sweet mate," he growled,

laying her down and teasing her with his whisper light kisses and gentle hands.

She didn't want him to be gentle. She wanted him rough and fierce, like he was when he'd defended her tonight. Boldly, she reached for him, taking two hands to encircle his girthy length. She squeezed and stroked, loving the helpless groan that escaped his lips at her ministrations.

Sexy, sexy mate.

"Mine," Derrick growled and crouched over her body on all fours.

"Show me," she demanded, lifting her arms wide and running her hands up his forearms to his biceps, and then his massive shoulders, skimming the top of his back, touching the tattoo that branded him as hers forever.

"I want one like yours," she said suddenly, stopping him short.

"What?"

"A tattoo. I want one too," she replied.

Derrick's eyes glowed gold and for a second she thought he would refuse, then a smile broke out on his face, and he was crushing his body and mouth to hers. Pleasure blossomed everywhere he touched. Arousal spiked, need grew, and love, so much love flared to life that it left Lucy breathless. He moved so slow, too slow, she tried bucking her hips, but he was immovable.

"Patience, mate," he growled deep and low, and her whole body quaked.

It was like his voice had a direct line to her clit, the needy little bud throbbed and twitched, practically begging for his touch.

"Gonna go slow, but I'll tell you what I'm going to do as I do it, okay? You want that, mate?"

Lucy nodded.

"Tell me."

"Yes, I want that. Please," she pleaded.

Hell, she was begging already, and he hadn't even started yet. Lucy didn't care. She wanted him more than she wanted to breathe.

"First, I'm going to lick your nipples, suck your breasts into my mouth," he growled and lifted her breasts in both hands, kneading the flesh and pinching her just enough till he sucked one plump mound into his hot mouth.

Her pussy throbbed, moisture flooding between her legs as he continued to tend to her breasts. Lucy begged, but he wouldn't budge. Only when he was satisfied did he lift his head.

"Got to taste you, mate. Gonna lick this pussy

until you're ready for me. Want that? Want me to lick your pretty pink pussy?"

"Yes, Derrick, yes," she moaned as he slid down her overheated body, licking a trail from her navel to her inner thigh as he went.

Derrick pushed her legs open, his face level with her sex, and just looked. Lucy felt exposed. So open and vulnerable, but she trusted her mate to take care of her.

"Look at you, so wet and ready, kitten. So mine," he growled, then dipped his head, spearing her heat with his long tongue.

"This is mine," he growled and spread her lips open with his fingers, sliding his digits across her swollen flesh. "You are all mine, kitten. Say it."

"Yours," she moaned with no more prompting.

She was desperate for him. Lucy could hardly think with wanting. She needed his mouth on her, his hands, his cock filling her. Now. But he was in no rush. She watched the smile spread across his face as he took his time teasing her. Derrick's fingers lightly breached her opening while his lips dropped soft kisses to her weeping slit. Finally, his gloriously rough tongue snaked out, and he lapped oh-so-slowly at her.

One stroke, then two. A finger. Then two. A graze. A nip. Another lick.

Fuck. Fuck. FUCK.

"Don't stop," she begged. She was so tense she could have snapped.

"Don't stop what?"

"Don't stop eating me," she moaned, rocking her hips to try to force those slick digits deeper inside of her, but he would not be budged. It was like he wanted her out of her mind with need.

"Love your taste, mate. This is my cream, isn't it? My pussy. And it tastes so good."

His tongue moved faster, with longer, harder swipes. Lucy couldn't be still. She bucked her hips, fucking his face with gusto, riding the wave of pleasure until she was screaming his name. When his head finally emerged, she was completely wrung out. Didn't think she had it in her to do more than blink and breathe.

"Mine."

His husky growl sent shockwaves of pleasure through her sex, and she throbbed with need renewed. He slid his hand out of her and brought the soaked digits to his mouth. One by one, he sucked them clean while she watched. Was there anything sexier?

"Need you," she said and reached for him, but still he would not be rushed.

Derrick slid slowly up her body until he was perfectly aligned with her heat.

"Watch baby, I want you to see how we become one. Mine," he lifted his chest and stomach so that she could see the view of his cock kissing her velvet wetness.

"Mine," she echoed, and felt her fangs lengthen and claws extend. She knew she pierced his skin with them as she pulled, but still her mate would not be rushed.

Inch by inch, he slid inside her until he filled her to the brim. So fucking hot and hard and heavy, his length stroked places she never even knew existed deep inside her.

"Fuck, you drive me wild, kitten. Love you. Mate. Mine. Mine. MINE!" he shouted in time with his moves.

Slam, withdraw, slam, withdraw.

Before they'd made love with the new wonder of mates finally meeting, but this was different. This was raw, dirty, Shifter fucking, and Lucy loved it.

"Gonna fuck you till you can't move," he snarled through his own fangs and she could see the Wolf in his eyes.

"Yes," she said, wanting it, needing it, needing him to confirm that they had both survived.

They were both here. Together. Harder and faster, Derrick pumped inside of her. Sex was good, she realized. She'd never trusted it, never wanted it before, but she would always want it with him. Sex with her mate was fucking amazing.

"Derrick, need, please," she growled, the need to come building and building until she was bucking and moving in earnest.

"I got what you need," he roared and flipped her onto her knees.

Ass out, he pressed her head down and spread her cheeks, teasing her hole before slamming his thick, long, glorious cock deep within her pussy. Derrick dropped forward, caging her in with his enormous body as he pounded her slick heat from behind.

"Come for me," he growled, and she wanted to.

She really did. So close. Almost there. He reached around with his thumb and found her clit. Strumming that tiny little nub, he flicked and fucked until she was hissing and roaring like the animal she was.

Pure bliss thundered through her as his cum filled her inside. He squeezed her ass with one hand

and thrust again, egging a second slower, but just as powerful orgasm to rush through her.

"So beautiful, mate," he grunted and withdrew from her, covering her with his arms even as she turned into him. They lay like that for hours, unable to move or speak, only capable of breathing and holding each other close.

"I love you, Derrick."

"Love you, mate. Mine," he answered.

"My home," she returned, and his responding smile was all the affirmation she needed.

EPILOGUE

"Are you shitting me?" Sheila practically howled with outrage as Detective Leo Crowley walked into *Serious Moonlight* and took his usual table in the dining room.

Now that they'd started opening early for lunch, they'd been seeing a lot more of the Lion Shifter, much to his baby cousin's consternation. Derrick nodded at the cop and winked at his cousin even as she grumbled and snatched a menu from Susan, the new human server and bartender they'd recently hired.

After the attack, the community really seemed to rally together, and support for *Serious Moonlight* was booming. Of course, they did not know about the supernatural world, but no one liked a terrorist and that was how the public viewed the attack as a war against a friendly MC that had been ostracized and mislabeled by the townies. No one wanted to be seen as politically incorrect these days, so yeah, they had more customers than ever. Either way, things were good.

"Derrick! Where are you?"

He turned as the front door opened and his mate strode in. His eyes went right to her stomach and the beast in him rumbled. True, her belly was only slightly swollen, but he couldn't help the possessive way he watched her. She was carrying their cubs, and he'd never seen anything so damn beautiful.

"Hey there, kitten. I'm here. Where you off to in such a huff?"

He lifted her to him and dropped a kiss on her mouth, loving the blush that spread across her face and the way her purple eyes glittered with her Cat. The sassy little feline was always asserting herself, especially in bed, and fuck, if he didn't love it.

"Derrick, Cole got Buddy towed here from Big Tom's, and now he's saying the car can't be fixed!"

"Now, darlin'," he began, trying to figure out how to broach the subject with his mate.

He'd wanted, no, he'd needed to make sure she was safe and driving that little junker with his cubs was just not happening.

"I see. So, you went and did this, didn't you?" she asked.

"Now, Lucy, I just want you safe, all of you," he explained. Picking her up so he could swipe his tongue across her lips.

Fuck, he loved it when her little pink appendage came out to play with his. The woman had one magical tongue. Matched the rest of her.

Lucky Alpha. Lucky man.

"Well, that's fine, I suppose. But I have an appointment at the doctor's office, so I guess I'll just take your wheels."

She'd been kissing him so sweetly, he didn't notice her hands searching his back pockets. By the time he did, she'd already snagged the keys to his bike and was jiggling them. Brain still foggy, thinking of ways he was going to make his mate scream his name, Derrick didn't move until he heard the roar of his twin engines come to life outside the bar.

"What the? Lucy!" he bellowed.

He was already too late. Pregnant and all, by the

time Derrick ran outside, it was to see his sassy mate speeding off down the highway on his Harley.

Fucking hell.

He looked around the lot, sensing he was all alone, and ran to the woods, shucking his clothes and bundling them into the knapsack he had stored there. With the straps secure in his mouth, he shifted to his Wolf and started pounding the asphalt to catch up to her. Hopefully, she'd wait inside her doc's office for him to dress and meet up with her. With a short howl, he pushed his legs harder. Fuck, he loved her. She was his match in every way.

No buts about it.

Derrick growled and used his power to run faster. If he wanted to catch his quick little mate, he needed to shake that sass.

Afterwards, he was taking her car shopping.

T*he end.*

Liked this story? Want more Dire Wolf Mates?
Grab the next book, Breaking Sass, at
https://www.cdgorri.com/books/breaking-sass.

Or

Follow the whole series at

https://www.cdgorri.com/seres/dire-wolf-mates.

Thank you and happy reading!

HAVE YOU MET THE BARVALE CLAN BEARS?

Looking for a Paranormal Romance series that is loads of growly fun?

Meet the Barvale Clan first in the Bear Claw Tales! A complete shifter romance series about 4 brothers who discover and need to win their fated mates!
Titles are:
Bearly Breathing
Bearly There
Bearly Tamed
Bearly Mated

Followed by two more spin off series, the Barvale Clan Tales, featuring:
Polar Opposites

Polar Outbreak
Polar Compound
Polar Curve

and, of course, the Barvale Holiday Tales:
A Bear For Christmas
Hers to Bear
Thank You Beary Much
Bearing Gifts

Look for more of these sexy, heartwarming holiday inspired tales soon!

No cliffhangers. Steamy PNR fun.
Go and read your next happily ever after today!

BEWARE... HERE BE DRAGONS!

The Falk Clan Tales are my stories surrounding four Dragon Shifter brothers and how they find their one true mates!

Each brother's chest is marked with his rose, the magical link to his heart and his magic. They each have a matching gemstone to go with it.

In *The Dragon's Valentine* we meet the eldest Falk brother, Callius. He is on a mission to find a Castle and his one true mate, one he can trust with his diamond rose....

She's given up on love, but he's just begun...

In *The Dragon's Christmas Gift* our attention shifts to Alexsander, the youngest brother of the four. He has resigned himself to a life alone, until he meets *her...*

His heart is frozen. Can she change his mind about love?

The Dragon's Heart is the story of Edric Falk who has vowed never to love again, but that changes when he meets his feisty mate, Joselyn Curacao.

Some wounds run deep. Can a Dragon's heart be unbroken?

Meet Nikolai Falk in the last Falk Clan Tale, *The Dragon's Secret.*

She just wants a little fun, he's looking for a lifetime.

*These first four books are now available in one convenient set. Look for Dragon Mates today. Now available in Paperback & Hardcover.

Meet another long lost Falk brother in *The Dragon's Treasure.* Castor Falk breaks free from his prison in search of his kin, he finds his mate instead.

She doesn't believe in fairytales, until a Dragon comes knocking on her door.

The Dragon's Surprise features a new Dragon, Devine Graystone, and a female Werewolf who makes him think twice about his lonely state of being…

Nothing can surprise this six hundred-year-old Dragon, except maybe her.

Lastly, in *The Dragon's Dream* we meet a spunky she-Wolf who gives Nicholas Graystone a run for his money when it comes to romance. Can a Dragon really have it all?

He's a hardcore realist until she dares him to dream.

OTHER TITLES BY C.D. GORRI

Other Titles by C.D. Gorri

Paranormal Romance Books:

Macconwood Pack Novel Series:

Charley's Christmas Wolf: A Macconwood Pack Novel 1

Cat's Howl: A Macconwood Pack Novel 2

Code Wolf: A Macconwood Pack Novel 3

The Witch and The Werewolf: A Macconwood Pack Novel 4

To Claim a Wolf: A Macconwood Pack Novel 5

Conall's Mate: A Macconwood Pack Novel 6

Her Solstice Wolf: A Macconwood Pack Novel 7

Werewolf Fever: A Macconwood Pack Novel 8

Also available in 2 boxed sets:

The Macconwood Pack Volume 1

The Macconwood Pack Volume 2

Macconwood Pack Tales Series:

Wolf Bride: The Story of Ailis and Eoghan A

Macconwood Pack Tale 1

Summer Bite: A Macconwood Pack Tale 2

His Winter Mate: A Macconwood Pack Tale 3

Snow Angel: A Macconwood Pack Tale 4

Charley's Baby Surprise: A Macconwood Pack Tale 5

Home for the Howlidays: A Macconwood Pack Tale 6

A Silver Wedding: A Macconwood Pack Tale 7

Mine Furever: A Macconwood Pack Tale 8

A Furry Little Christmas: A Macconwood Pack Tale 9

Also available in two boxed sets:

The Macconwood Pack Tales Volume 1

Shifters Furever: The Macconwood Pack Tales Volume 2

<u>The Falk Clan Tales:</u>

The Dragon's Valentine: A Falk Clan Novel 1

The Dragon's Christmas Gift: A Falk Clan Novel 2

The Dragon's Heart: A Falk Clan Novel 3

The Dragon's Secret: A Falk Clan Novel 4

The Dragon's Treasure: A Falk Clan Novel 5

The Dragon's Surprise: A Falk Clan Novel 6

The Dragon's Dream: A Falk Clan Novel 7

Dragon Mates: The Falk Clan Series Boxed Set Books 1-4

<u>The Bear Claw Tales:</u>

Bearly Breathing: A Bear Claw Tale 1

Bearly There: A Bear Claw Tale 2

Bearly Tamed: A Bear Claw Tale 3

Bearly Mated: A Bear Claw Tale 4

Also available in a boxed set:

The Complete Bear Claw Tales (Books 1-4)

<u>The Barvale Clan Tales:</u>

Polar Opposites: The Barvale Clan Tales 1

Polar Outbreak: The Barvale Clan Tales 2

Polar Compound: A Barvale Clan Tale 3

Polar Curve: A Barvale Clan Tale 4

Also available in a boxed set:

The Barvale Clan Tales (Books 1-4)

<u>Barvale Holiday Tales:</u>

A Bear For Christmas

Hers To Bear

Thank You Beary Much

Bearing Gifts

Also available in a boxed set:

The Barvale Holiday Tales (Books 1-3)

<u>Purely Paranormal Romance Books:</u>

Marked by the Devil: Purely Paranormal Romance Books

Mated to the Dragon King: Purely Paranormal Romance Books

Claimed by the Demon: Purely Paranormal Romance Books

Christmas with a Devil, a Dragon King, & a Demon: Purely Paranormal Romance Books

Vampire Lover: Purely Paranormal Romance Books

Grizzly Lover: Purely Paranormal Romance Books

Christmas With Her Chupacabra: Purely Paranormal Romance Books

Purely Paranormal Romance Books Anthology

The Wardens of Terra:

Bound by Air: The Wardens of Terra Book 1

Star Kissed: A Wardens of Terra Short

Waterlocked: The Wardens of Terra Book 2

Moon Kissed: A Wardens of Terra Short

*Now in a boxed set and in audio!

The Maverick Pride Tales:

Purrfectly Mated

Purrfectly Kissed

Purrfectly Trapped

Purrfectly Caught

Purrfectly Naughty

Purrfectly Bound

<u>Howl's Romance</u>

Mated to the Werewolf Next Door: A Howl's Romance

The Tiger King's Christmas Bride

Claiming His Virgin Mate: Howls Romance

<u>Twice Mated Tales</u>

Doubly Claimed

Doubly Bound

Doubly Tied

<u>Hearts of Stone Series</u>

Shifter Mountain: Hearts of Stone 1

Shifter City: Hearts of Stone 2

Shifter Village: Hearts of Stone 3

<u>Accidentally Undead Series</u>

Fangs For Nothin'

<u>Moongate Island Tales</u>

Moongate Island Mate

Moongate Island Christmas Claim

<u>Mated in Hope Falls</u>

Mated by Moonlight

<u>Speed Dating with the Denizens of the Underworld</u>

Ash: Speed Dating with the Denizens of Underworld

Arachne: Speed Dating with the Denizens of Underworld

Hungry Fur Love

Hungry Like Her Wolf: Magic and Mayhem Universe

Hungry For Her Bear: Magic and Mayhem Universe

Shifters Unleashed Boxed Sets

Check out these amazing anthologies where you can find some of my books and the works of other awesome authors!

Midnight Magic Anthology (Water Witch)

Rituals & Runes Anthology (Air Witch)

Island Stripe Pride

Tiger Claimed

Tiger Denied

NYC Shifter Tales

Cuff Linked

Sealed Fate

A Howlin' Good Fairytale Retelling

Sweet As Candy (as seen in Once Upon An Ever After)

Coming Soon:

Asterion

Vampire Shield: Guardians of Chaos 6

Tiger Rejected

For Fangs Sake

Hungry As Her Python: Magic and Mayhem Universe

If The Shoe Fits: A Howlin' Good Fairytale Retelling

Chickee and the Paparazzi: FUCN'A

The Wolf's Winter Wish: A Macconwood Pack Tale

The Hybrid Assassin

Tempted By Her Protector: WPU 2

Alien Protector: WPU 3

Elvish Protector: WPU 4

Thrilled By Her Protector: WPU 5

<u>Young Adult Urban Fantasy Books:</u>

Wolf Moon: A Grazi Kelly Novel Book 1

Hunter Moon: A Grazi Kelly Novel Book 2

Rebel Moon: A Grazi Kelly Novel Book 3

Winter Moon: A Grazi Kelly Novel Book 4

Chasing The Moon: A Grazi Kelly Short 5

Blood Moon: A Grazi Kelly Novel 6

*Get all 6 books NOW AVAILABLE IN A BOXED SET:

The Complete Grazi Kelly Novel Series

Casting Magic: The Angela Tanner Files 1

Keeping Magic: The Angela Tanner Files 2

<u>G'Witches Magical Mysteries Series</u>

Co-written with P. Mattern

G'Witches

G'Witches 2: The Harpy Harbinger

G'Witches 3: Summoning Secrets

EXCERPT FROM PURRFECTLY MATED

How the fuck did I wind up here?

It was all Elissa could do not to slam her face down on the table as she pondered that question for the umpteenth time since leaving her cozy Hoboken apartment to go on this so called date.

"So, babe," the over-stuffed, heavily-cologned, and downright fugly man said.

Her date of the evening looked like something out of a bad sitcom as he tried to lean over the stained tablecloth of the rundown hotel buffet room, he'd driven two hours to get to. Waggling his caterpillar-like eyebrows, he gave her the once over and Elissa's skin crawled.

Oh, hell no.

"I got a room upstairs, you know, for *after*," he told her, nodding his head, and biting his lower lip in a manner she assumed he thought was provocative.

At best, it was nauseating.

FML.

How was this guy Elissa's date for the evening? What had she done to deserve this?

Little Gianni. Yup, that was how he'd introduced himself. And here she was. On a blind date with a guy who had the word 'little' in front of his name.

Well, what did she expect? Roses and champagne? In this economy? She didn't know where Cinder-fucking-ella got her prince, but it sure as fuck wasn't in Jersey.

Elissa could only blame herself for agreeing to go on this blind date. Initially, the whole Little Gianni fiasco had been intended for her roommate.

Wait a second. Scratch that thought.

It *was* all Gretchen's fault. That ungrateful cow!

She tried to play it off like she was some sweet little homegrown maiden. Oh, just wait till Elissa got home. Gretchen was never going to hear the end of it.

She owed Elissa. Big time. Like a whole month of

washing the dishes big time. The rat trap they shared in her hometown of Hoboken was all the two women could afford, and for the most part, they got along just fine.

In fact, they'd grown to be close friends over the three years they'd lived together. It was the only reason she'd ever agreed to this date from Hell.

Elissa sighed and looked over at Little Gianni. Maybe he wasn't all that bad?

"*BEEEELLLLLLLLCHHH!* 'Scuse me, doll. Better out, am I right?"

Gianni winked and Elissa wished for a black hole to open up and swallow her up right through the floor.

OMFG.

The man just burped out loud like he was in a frat boy belting contest, only those days passed him up about thirty years ago.

For fuck's sake. Gretchen, you so owe me.

Elissa cursed her roommate and tried not to groan. But Little Gianni wasn't quite done. The grown ass man lifted his leg and let one rip.

Right. Fucking. There.

Elissa was going to die before the end of the night.

Literally.

This is what you get when you do a friend a favor without asking for details! Idiota!

The voice of her Italian grandmother sounded in her brain. She tried to ignore it, willing herself not to wince at the man while he sucked air, and who knows what else, noisily through his coffee-stained teeth.

Ew. So gross.

That was the perfect word to describe it. The only word, in fact. The entire date was just so fucking gross. She still couldn't believe her sweet little roommate from Iowa, *Gretchen Kaepernick*, she of the wispy hair and baby blues, had set her up with this guy!

What the actual fuck was up with that?

Little Gianni was a slob. Actually, he looked just like her Uncle Nico, and that was not a good thing. Seriously, not good at all.

He wore his hair slicked back in a too tight ponytail that emphasized his rapidly receding hairline. As if that wasn't enough to put her off, he was sporting an enormous paunch. Now, being a curvy girl, Elissa appreciated food and was in no way against men showing the same appreciation.

She liked bigger men. Always had. But bigger did not mean you had to be sloppy. Little Gianni's stomach was literally hanging out from under a tight tan golf shirt that had definitely seen better days.

The man didn't even look like he had ever played a sport of any kind. With it, he wore brown polyester pants that were three inches above his ankles and unbuttoned at the waist.

He didn't look like he tried at all for this date. What kind of guy did that? His shirt collar was bent and wrinkled, and all three buttons were open to his chest, revealing a mat of oily, dark hair and pimples.

Somehow, he'd managed to tuck the back of the shirt in, but the front simply would not hold in that stomach. What worried her more were the tight brown pants.

As he sat back and stretched, she wondered if she should take cover. They looked like they were one bite from exploding off his body. Elissa shuddered at the image.

Please God, if You have an ounce of mercy, don't let that happen, she prayed.

"Hang on, doll, I gotta take this," he said, and turned to answer his cell phone.

It was ringing to the tune of '70s disco music she

hadn't heard since the last family reunion. Her eyes kept going to the huge stain on the front of his shirt. It was a little game she liked to call *what the hell is that.*

Coffee, she guessed.

"Up your ass, Bruno. I gotta have it by Monday," he cursed into the receiver.

Elissa winced at the spectacle he was making of them both. There were only a handful of people there, but still.

Deep breaths.

Ew. Maybe not.

She coughed as the strong body spray, that he'd obviously used a ton of in lieu of a shower, bad move in her opinion, invaded her lungs.

Oh, this was so bad.

Elissa was, by no means, a snob. But this guy looked like he'd stepped out of a bad 1980s mafia spoof film. What's worse, he kept smacking his lips together as he hung up the phone and looked her over from head to chest.

Thank fuck for the table, she thought, wishing she could hide her bosoms from his view.

"Ssssss," he hissed, like it was sexy or something.

She just grimaced. Elissa might be able to forgive a lot of quirks, but she hated mouth noises. Really hated them. It was a super pet peeve of hers. Never mind his totally inappropriate and unwelcomed leer.

She started counting the minutes, willing the date to be over already. Plenty of people would tell her she shouldn't be so choosy, but really? She was not this desperate.

Not yet anyway.

So, she was curvy and a little mouthy too. But was it wrong to want a man with good table manners? Even if men were thin on the ground for someone like her.

As a chef, she'd worked in a lot of restaurants and even as a personal cook for professional couples. She'd seen her fair share of unhappy couples and downright uncomfortable marriages. But as far as she was concerned, all relationships went downhill when good table manners were dismissed.

Good manners were merely a sign that a person was thoughtful and respectful. At least, that was what Nonna had told her. Gianni here had clearly missed that lesson as a child. Elissa had to work not to groan in disgust as he slurped a raw clam down his gullet.

Shudder.

Was there no end to his feeding? That's what it reminded her of. Feeding time at the zoo.

OMG. That was rude, she scolded herself. But it wasn't like she said it out loud.

All she wanted to do was go home. At least she was comfortable. *She'd* worn her softest pair of black leggings for this disaster date, paired with one of her favorite tunics on top.

It was dark green with tiny black buttons down the front and showed just the right amount of cleavage. She'd gone for neat and tidy as opposed to downright sexy.

Good call, in her opinion. Elissa looked perfectly fine for a nice *getting to know you* dinner, which is what she thought she was getting when her roommate asked her to step in for her on a blind date that one of her best client's had set up for her.

Elissa shuddered now, thinking how good old Gianni here would've reacted to the red dress and heels she'd contemplated before checking the weather report.

Gulp.

The lewd man was already salivating, and she was so not having it. Fending off his unwanted advances was not how she wanted to finish the night.

Ew again.

Elissa shivered, slightly chilled despite the fact

they were indoors. It was a cold, gloomy evening, and the forecast called for even more rain later that night. Not at all unusual for this time of year in the Garden State.

November was always chilly in the evenings, rainy too. Elissa tended to run warm, but she was glad she'd brought a jacket with her. Especially since her date refused to turn the heat on in the car.

When she'd asked, he'd looked offended and told her it wasted gas.

Um. Okay.

She checked her phone. It was only seven o'clock, but the two hour drive was still ahead of them. Maybe they could make it home before ten if they left soon.

Ugh. Did he just blow his nose?

"Allergies, doll. Say, you gonna eat that?" he asked before scooping a fry from her dish and swallowing it down.

Elissa was gonna kill her roomie. Gretchen was a hair and nail stylist. A lot of her clients were elderly, and they just loved her. They were always offering to set her up on blind dates with their nephews and grandsons.

Mostly, the sweet old ladies were kind. They swore they could find her curvy roommate the right man, assuming she was single because she was new to town. Well, when Elissa got home tonight, she was going to tell Gretchen she needed to fire the old lady who set this date up from being her client.

Like *ASAP*.

No one who liked Gretchen would've sent her out with this guy. Gianni reached over and touched her hand and Elissa pulled back, reaching for the napkin.

Gross.

"I sure hope you ain't a cold one, doll," he said, shaking his head.

"What?"

"Ain't gonna matter. I know just what you need, doll."

She was still wiping the greasy residue he'd transferred to her skin from the food he ate sans utensils. This was too much. Elissa was beyond uncomfortable with all the leering and bad attempts at innuendo.

Plus, she was starving. One look at the dump he'd taken her to, and she knew she could never eat there. The chef in her wouldn't allow it.

To think they drove two hours for this! She'd practically frozen to death in his maroon Cadillac, listening to a CD of the Rat Pack, while Gianni crooned loudly, and off key, to the music.

Normally, she was a fan of the famous group of legendary singers. Having grown up in Hoboken, she couldn't not be a Sinatra fan. Though, to be honest, Dean Martin had always been her favorite.

Still, Elissa was a firm believer that there were just some people you did not try to imitate. Especially not if you were Little Gianni. While he was belting his heart out, he'd been trying to get his right hand on her thigh. She'd asked him politely to stop.

Twice.

Then she'd been forced to try something a little more drastic. Like spilling her hot tea on the offending hand the third time he'd tried it. Finally, he'd removed his hand from her leg. Not making a fourth attempt, which she was grateful for.

Elissa should've taken that behavior as a sign and gotten out of the car. But no. She'd wanted to do Gretchen a solid. So, against her better judgement, she gave the creep another chance.

Idiota, her grandmother's voice echoed in her brain again.

The old woman had loved her. Elissa knew that without a doubt. She'd raised her after her own parents had passed on in a tragic automobile accident when Elissa was just twelve.

Her grandmother was a no-nonsense kind of lady who dished out priceless wisdom with brutally honest insights. It was the same way she dished out huge bowls of pasta with her amazing meatballs and homemade sauce. Not to mention a side order of back-breaking hugs that Elissa still missed.

Nonna cooked like that all the time. She made a huge pot of sauce every weekend, and she was happy to serve it to Elissa and her teammates and friends, especially after games and tournaments.

Soccer had been her sport of choice, and cooking had soon become her favorite hobby. Her grandmother had encouraged her in both pursuits. Guiding her in one and cheering her on in the other. Elissa still missed her terribly.

"Hey babe, ain't you gonna eat nothin'? You know they charge twenty dollars just to sit down," Little Gianni interrupted her train of thought.

Elissa was forced to turn her mind back to the present, which unfortunately included watching, *and hearing,* him as he sucked on his teeth and stuffed another breaded shrimp down his throat.

"I'm fine," she answered with a polite smile plastered on her face.

Just get home, Lissa. Just get him to take you home.

Elissa closed her eyes when he looked back down at his dish. Thank God for small favors, she mused. At least he was more interested in eating at the moment.

He'd taken her to the rattiest looking hotel and casino she'd ever seen in her life. And the buffet room?

Ew.

Seriously, the place had to be violating at least a dozen health codes. When Gianni had said Atlantic City, she'd thought at least the atmosphere would be exciting. But they were so far from the real glitz and entertainment, they might as well be anywhere else.

She sighed, looking at the plate she'd made for herself. Elissa couldn't even fake an interest in the food. As a chef, it was hard enough to dine out.

She was always judging the food, the service, the ingredients. How could she not? It was her business. And that was when the food was good!

This was not good. Not at all.

She'd been to hospitals that served better food. Old yellow lights buzzed and blinked around the buffet, giving it an abandoned kind of feel. The menu was made up of mostly frozen then fried or baked cuisine.

Reheated actually. It was like a giant TV dinner buffet where every item was previously frozen when already cooked and warmed up in an oven.

It was the kind of food sold cheap at restaurant supply stores in bulk. Yeah, this was much worse than hospital food, in her opinion.

There was a worn carpet on the floor, a handful of scattered tables in the dining room, elevator music on in the background, and the entire place smelled like canned soup.

Not to mention not one of the five people there besides them was under sixty years old.

"Gianni," she said, leaning forward so as not to hurt his feelings.

"I thought you mentioned something about seeing a show tonight. Is it here?"

Please don't be here.

If he was taking her somewhere else, she could beg off and hire a cab to take her home. There was no way she was sitting through anything else with this man. Not now. Not ever.

"Ah, I see, babe, you want some entertainment first, I get it," he snickered loudly, and she blanched.

Whatever he thought was going to happen wasn't. She needed to disabuse him of the notion, and fast.

"Alright, alright. Lemme finish this, babe. Then we'll go up to the room I got for us," he said.

Before she could make sense of the ludicrous statement, he slurped another fried shrimp, don't ask how. Then he grabbed her arm and yanked her from the seat before she could even react.

Elissa tugged on his hold, but the man was immovable. Tossing a five-dollar bill on the table, Little Gianni snatched a toothpick from the hostess stand before dragging her outside.

Great, he was a cheap tipper, too.

All she wanted was to go home. Figuring the best way to do that would probably be to get him to the car, she let him lead the way.

Once inside, she would ask him to drive back to Hoboken so she could wring Gretchen's neck. Fuming, she pulled her arm out of his hand and walked behind him.

The rain was really pouring, and the cheap bastard had refused valet. Elissa ducked her head so she wouldn't get so wet. Of course, the jacket she'd brought was light and had no hood.

Gianni had an umbrella, but he didn't offer to hold it for her, and honestly, she did not relish the idea of getting any closer to him than necessary.

Seriously, not happening.

Now all she had to do was break the news. She had no intention of watching a show or returning to the hotel with him.

What could go wrong?

GRAB PURRFECTLY MATED TODAY.

EXCERPT FROM WOLF SHIELD

"Why are we traipsing through the fucking swamp to meet your so-called contact, Fur?" Hudson Stormwolfe, or Storm as he was known, growled at his friend and fellow Guardian, "a goddamn coffee shop wouldn't do?"

The Horse Shifter snorted as Storm stepped in a hole cursing quietly as a trickle of slimy sludge slipped inside his once clean steel-toed boots.

"Oh, you are going to scrape these clean," he shot at Furio.

"Dude, just watch your step," Furio retorted making a show of how easily his long legs ate up the muddy landscape.

Fuck him, snarled Storm's Wolf. Trudging through the muck was not his animal's idea of a good time. Give him a dense, clean forest any day. Storm only agreed to accompany Furio because Kingston told him to go.

Their leader could be a hard ass at times, but no one fucked with the Dragon Shifter just lately. Not because they were afraid, but for other reasons. Losing one's mate could really fuck a guy up inside. Besides, Storm had liked Neela, may she rest in peace for eternity.

Damn the Loyalists. Those bastards were nothing more than terrorists and fanatics attacking supernatural creatures and hoarding magic for their own nefarious purposes. They wanted to control and siphon out the one thing every supernatural needed to live with their leaders as the gatekeepers. That thing was of course magic itself.

Loyalists believed that common folk had no business accessing magic. They wanted to keep it for the elite, the wealthy, and basically anyone who did what they said. They were nothing more than pirates and madmen as far as Storm was concerned.

They had been around for nearly as long as the Guardians of Chaos. Storm was proud to call himself a Guardian. He was more than able and willing to do his part to ensure freedom for all supernatural-kind.

Even after all this time, those bastards still failed to gain the momentum necessary to achieve their goals. Their terroristic acts were the stuff of nightmares. Especially this latest attack on the Guardians' leader. The heinous crime was without precedent.

It still left a bad taste in Storm's mouth. He gritted his teeth as his mind still tried to take in the fact she was gone. Neela Baldric, the beloved mate of their once fearless leader, was brutally attacked while on her way to the supermarket.

The gentlewoman was a rare and precious creature and was mated to his superior, Kingston Baldric, for many years. She'd only just succumbed to her wounds a few months ago, leaving all of them bereft of her company, but none so much as Kingston.

"We all miss her, bro," Furio said, and Storm realized he'd been projecting.

Fuck. He hated it when he did that. Though truthfully, it wouldn't have mattered. Furio felt her loss as well. Everyone in Kingston's group of Guardians felt the loss keenly.

These kinds of terroristic acts were the new tool the Loyalists used to persuade mainstream paranormal society to their way of thinking. Blackmail, bribery, murder, mayhem, all elements of destruction that this so-called law-abiding organization stooped to in order to fulfill their aims.

Not on his watch, Storm vowed to himself. It was his job and that of all the Guardians to stop those bastards and ensure freedom for their kind.

"Sorry," Storm muttered, "still, we had to meet in a fucking swamp, Furio?"

"What swamp, bro? We're in Secaucus," Furio opened his arms wide and gestured to the thick, musty smelling wetland they were currently stalking through.

It was just a little past ten o'clock at night, but summer in the Garden State meant hot and sticky. Especially in that small portion of undeveloped marshlands. Storm growled when his foot sank yet again, ankle-deep, into another muddy hole.

Goddamn it, he grimaced, and slapped his friend in the back of the head. Then he counted to three like he'd been told to do by another of their own, Egros, a male Witch who thought the Wolf Shifter would have better control if he could simply manage his anger.

Yeah. Right. The hell with counting. He was going to kick Furio's ass when they were done here.

"Half the fucking state is a swamp," Storm

growled, shaking the muck off his foot, "I thought you were born here?"

"I was. Born and bred in Hoboken, *cumpy*."

"What?"

"Nothin' man, just some local slang from when I was a kid. Anyway, you're shittin' me right, New Jersey isn't a swamp," snorted the Stallion Shifter.

Storm rolled his eyes and blew out a breath. What was he going to do with this guy? Thirty years as a Guardian, and Furio was still a rookie to Storm, who'd spoke his vows over a hundred years ago this past April.

As a Wolf Shifter, he had a longer than average life expectancy, which had only increased when he'd pledged his allegiance to serve all the supernatural creatures living on this planet as a Guardian. He'd fought too many battles to count, but the work was meaningful. Protecting freedom always was.

It had been the same for his grandfather, who'd raised him just outside the boundaries of the Pack where his father still ruled as Alpha. His older brother was the heir which usually meant younger brothers were ousted or had to challenge for positions in the Pack. Rather than stay and fight for his dominance in the place of his birth, he'd left.

Storm respected tradition, but he had had a

higher calling to serve. The Guardians of Chaos were an elite order of supernaturals. The higher ups did not want it said they were showing favoritism to any specific Pack, Clan, Coven or what have you, so they composed each unit of a mix of *supes*. It took years to build the kind of team Storm was a part of.

Furio might be considered new, but he was still one of them. So fine, maybe Storm wouldn't kick his ass outright, but he could best him in training. That would satisfy both his Wolf and human sides.

"Did you hear Kingston has a meeting with the Assembly next week to discuss Neela's passing?" Furio spoke in a low voice, but with his supernaturally enhanced senses, Storm heard him just fine.

"I did. The Assembly, are all former Guardians, they will understand Kingston's loss and will likely support his call to mount a hunt for the Loyalist who'd ordered the hit," Storm responded.

"We're not Enforcers, Storm. Their job is to police the paranormal peoples of the earth, not ours. Guardians of Chaos don't promote actual chaos, right?" asked Furio, and he was right to a point.

"Look, we are called Guardians of Chaos, because from chaos, aka freedom, comes creativity. If we lose that, we perish. A Guardian is the ultimate protector of free thought, and therefore, the champion of creation itself. Neela was a cherished female and Kingston's to protect and to avenge. We might not understand what it is like to be mated, Furio, but he has rights and this did happen because of our war," Storm responded.

"All for magic? Neela was killed so the Loyalists could control magic? How would that even happen?"

"No, she was killed to break us. Without our leader, the Loyalists hope to win whatever scheme they are hatching and believe me, they are always plotting something. Whoever controls magic, controls us all," he grunted.

The way Storm understood it, magic was a finite thing, like ore, it was distributed organically, used, and recycled by each supernatural group as needed. The ancient ones, gods, goddesses, or what have you created magic out of chaos for each paranormal species to grow and take shape.

"What would they do, if they had it all?" Furio asked.

"What's with all the fucking questions?" growled Storm.

It was not for any one of them to control the others' usage of this gift. It went against their very nature as magical creatures.

Storm understood this. It was why he'd never

looked back after leaving the Black Moon Pack to follow in his grandfather's footsteps. With his father still ruling and his brother as heir, his life there would have been difficult to say the least.

He was too dominant. More so than his old man, yet the tradition dictated that the second son could not be Alpha.

Leaving was his only option, and his grandfather had ensured that he had all the knowledge he needed before his time came. Storm had joined the crusade against those who sought to rule over the entire supernatural world before he was old enough to vote. He knew his duty was no longer to Pack, but to his band of Guardians.

Which was why he was wading through the last thick patch of swampland left undeveloped in Secaucus, New Jersey, home of the best outlet shopping this side of the Hudson River for which he was named, at the behest of one of his own.

Fucking Furio.

"Sorry, *cump*, talking helps pass the time. Anyway, my CI prefers to be away from prying eyes, you know he's part Goblin, and more than a little skittish."

"Yeah, well, what news does he have, anyway?"

"He thinks he found the Loyalists' new headquarters. It was too good a tip to pass up. He's supposed to have the GPS coordinates for me tonight."

"Shit. That is important. But he couldn't have texted them?"

"Nah," Furio shook his head, causing his long hair, which was bound in a leather thong to sway side to side, mimicking that of his shifted form.

He stopped to touch one of the long overgrown cattails they'd passed, and Storm stilled in his tracks, wondering if he heard something. Like a woman breathing or humming or something. But how could that be? They were in the middle of nowhere. Furio dropped the cattail and turned toward the soft, and admittedly pleasant, vocals.

"Hey, you hear that?" Furio asked.

Storm raised his hand to quiet the other man. His Wolf was at full attention. A warm breeze blew in their direction, and he breathed it in deep siphoning through the various layers, hoping to identify whatever made that sound.

Along with the heavy scent of the dense and decaying vegetation, came another, lighter, much more pleasant fragrance. It sifted through Storm's highly acute olfactory system, teasing and tempting his senses. Whatever it was, Storm wanted more.

His Wolf's ears worked to zero in on the source

of both the sounds and the tantalizing fragrance that seemed too soft, too fine for the misty marshlands of Secaucus, New Jersey.

"It's like brown sugar and marzipan," he murmured as the sweet fragrance danced across his senses, like something out of a dream.

"What?" laughed Furio, but he ignored the Stallion.

He knew better than to go traipsing off after a phantom scent, but there was something about it. Something all too tempting and familiar. Storm's Wolf perked up. He growled low and deep as he took in another breath.

That scent, that crazy good scent, was like a shock to the system, but not necessarily unpleasant. More like an awakening. Storm noticed the Stallion Shifter walking through the thicket towards that divine fragrance, and the Wolf inside of him snarled.

"What the fuck, *cump*?" Furio asked.

Storm shook his head. What the fuck was wrong with him? Furio was his friend and fellow Guardian.

It didn't matter. It upset the Wolf. Storm shook his head and tried to silence the beast, but his animal was insistent. He needed to beat his friend to the source of that heavenly scent.

"Shit," he growled.

He hurried past the Stallion, using his superior height to gain the advantage, despite Furio's better speed. The Stallion couldn't beat him there. Storm would not allow it. He leapt over fallen trees and shrubs, avoiding the holes that had gotten him twice already in the deceptively soft, wet earth, until he reached the edge of what seemed to be a parking lot.

The heavy breathing coming from behind him told the Wolf that Furio had managed to keep pace, but the Stallion needed to hit the gym more if he was out of breath. It was shameful for a Guardian to be so easily exhausted. Then again, when had he ever beaten the Horse Shifter in a race?

"Damn, Storm, I never saw you run so fast," he huffed and Storm blinked in surprise, "shit, if I'd have known this lot was so close, I wouldn't have made us park behind the stadium and walk," the Stallion sucked in air greedily.

"Shhh," Storm held up his hand for silence.

His Wolf's enhanced vision allowed him to make out the details of the scene before him. They were just outside the fenced in parking lot of some kind of building. There was a municipal sign hanging up not too far away.

It was late at night, so it wasn't the courthouse, and there were no cop cars parked outside, so it wasn't a police station either. He looked around for any other indication of what the older cement building was. Ah, another dented sign.

"It's a library," Furio whispered.

"I see that," Storm growled.

He was angry and on edge, and he had no fucking idea why. His entire body vibrated with energy. He was not nervous, just impatient, he realized. That was odd, too.

What could he possibly be waiting for here? His Wolf dripped saliva from his fangs as he waited in that metaphysical plane where he rested until Storm called to him. He tried to consider what led him there, but all coherent thought fled his brain the second *she* came into view.

The strange woman was all the way on the other end of the tiny parking lot. A tall security fence and a good fifty feet of black asphalt stood between the female and the place where the two Guardians lurked, but Storm could still make out every detail of the stunning creature.

"She's a little round, but I always did like a girl with some cushion for the pushin'," Furio elbowed him jokingly, but his words enraged Storm.

The Wolf inside of him snarled and growled and before he could stop himself, he had Furio by the collar of his shirt. He'd lifted the Stallion a good foot off the ground before shock had him dropping his friend.

"The fuck?" Furio choked and rubbed his bruised neck.

Storm ignored him, eyes glued to the woman in the ankle-length skirt and short-sleeved blouse. She wore shiny red shoes with high spindle-like heels. *Stilettos*, he thought, and for the first time he understood why they were called that.

They might not be good for running, but the long, skinny heels could pierce a man's heart just like the stealthy blade someone named them after. As it was, he more than appreciated the way the shiny red heels lengthened her legs and caused her hips to sway seductively in the yellowish glow of the streetlights.

Her hair was pulled back in a loose bun. She'd obviously tried to tame her fiery red locks, but curls still fell around her lovely face. Storm observed the subtle highlights and lowlights in her hair color even in the diminished light, noting with pleasure her eyelashes held the same coppery tinge.

So, she was a natural redhead. Good. He did not like artificial things. Unlike most redheads who leaned towards fair-skinned, this beautiful woman had a healthy bronze glow to her. Her whiskey brown eyes were large and bright in the darkness.

He appreciated her plump pink lips, straight nose, and stubborn little chin. She was a knockout. The most gorgeous creature he'd ever laid eyes on.

Storm was thunderstruck. He watched her innocently sashay across the otherwise deserted parking lot to a beat up looking pick-up truck.

Hmm. Odd car choice, he thought.

That was all he had time to think as three men crept out of the shadows and circled the tiny female. Blood rushed through his being and he couldn't make out what was being said.

Whatever it was, didn't matter. One of them dared grab her arm and tossed her purse aside. Storm's fangs lengthened and claws popped free of his nails. The sound of her scream woke something furious inside of him. His entire body trembled with the strength of his fury. He needed to get to her. Now. There was no time to lose.

"Uh, what is that?" Furio tapped his shoulder and Storm turned and snarled.

His friend pointed down. Storm looked and took a step back in surprise. His palms were glowing. Small blue lights were circling both hands. His feet and legs were covered in what looked like shadowy black smoke billowing skywards. It was magic. He knew that much. It didn't hurt, but he'd never felt it before.

"Holy shit, Storm! Do you know what this means?"

Then it hit him. The reason for all the sudden changes. He turned to Furio and growled one word.

"Mine."

His female shrieked and hit the ground, and the Wolf inside him howled in fury.

Protect, the Wolf demanded.

He barely blinked his eyes, then he was directly in front of the female. It was like he'd moved through time and space. Storm appeared in front of her, shielding her from the soon-to-be-dead men who dared touch what was his.

He lifted his lip and snarled at the three assholes. It was nothing more than legend, he'd always thought. A fairy tale to keep younger *supes* from leaving the order. But he might have to change his mind.

He lifted his fists, still glowing with blue magic, and slammed it into the face of the first one of the three to launch an attack against him. Sparks flew, as did the assailant's teeth.

"What are you waiting for," Storm said to the other two.

He smiled wickedly. Looked like even Shifter fairy tales were true sometimes. It was rumored that the Guardians were blessed by the Fates that upon finding their true mates they would receive certain magical benefits to promote honoring their vows till death.

Stronger together, those were the words etched inside the doorway of the Keep. Now Storm finally understood their meaning.

"Mine," he looked down into startled butterscotch eyes.

He knew without doubt; the woman was his mate, and he would shield her from harm.

Always.

GRAB WOLF SHIELD TODAY.

EXCERPT FROM BEARING GIFTS

"Thanks for coming tonight, Charity," Abigail Jensen, a nurse who worked at the Barvale Senior Center spoke softly as Charity hung her coat and hat on the rack near the desk.

It was already snowing, and she only had a few minutes, but Abigail never called her if it wasn't an emergency. Charity just had a way with people, and she enjoyed spending her time helping put others at ease if she could. True, she had about fifteen minutes before she needed to leave on time, otherwise she would be late for her shift, and tonight was important.

"No worries. You know I enjoy spending time with the residents, Abigail."

"I know, but normally you come on the weekends. Mr. K is a special case, and we have tried everything to make him feel at ease. His wife had to have emergency hip replacement surgery, and he is only here while she recovers, but he's been despondent without her."

"Wow, he must really love her," Charity whispered. She shuffled the box that held a single bear claw inside and followed Abby down the hall. Seated in a wheelchair in the middle of his room was an elderly man with white hair and a beard. He had a hand-knitted red scarf draped around his neck, and his hands were clasped together.

"Good evening, Mr. K. I brought you a visitor," Abigail announced, and Charity walked in.

"Hello, I'm Charity—"

"I don't need any charity, I need my Elaine," he muttered grumpily.

"I understand. If I had a wife or husband, I would miss her too, but the center isn't all bad, you know. I usually come by on weekends and bring treats like this and crafts or movies. Sometimes, we play card games and once we had a talent show."

"A talent show? And what can you do, my dear?" he asked, engaging already, and Charity smiled at the win.

"Well, Mr. K, not to brag, but I am a terrible dancer, and I can't carry a tune," she confided.

"I will leave you two to it," Abigail said and turned to leave.

For the next fifteen minutes, Charity chatted with the exceedingly kind Mr. K, answering questions, and getting the older gentleman to open up about his wife. Her recovery was slow going, but he talked to her every single day. That kind of devotion was really touching, and Charity's heart swelled hoping someday, she would have that kind of love for herself.

"So, do you still believe in Santa?" he asked.

"Oh, I don't know. When I was little, I used to stay up and wait to hear him, but I never did. I think that would be amazing—"

"Even now that you are a grownup? I am surprised."

"Why? Adults need magic too," she told him.

"That is true, my dear. This was so lovely, Charity. Thank you for visiting me," Mr. K said, taking her hand as she stood to leave.

"It was my pleasure."

"You know, Christmas is in just a few days. I hope you sent your letter to Santa already," he whispered conspiratorially, and she laughed.

"I sure did," she replied, and kissed his weathered cheek.

"Oh, how nice! I am going to tell my Elaine she must get well faster, a younger woman has her sights on me," he teased.

"You do that, and I bet she will be better in no time. You are quite the catch, Mr. K!" Charity chuckled.

"Seriously, my child, I want to thank you, very much so. I do not know many young women who would stop by to chat with a grumpy old stranger."

"You're not grumpy, Mr. K, just sad, and it is understandable. I bet you're worried something awful about your wife, and I want you to know I will be praying for her speedy recovery. I am sorry to cut our talk short, though, but I have to go."

"I see. Hot date?" he asked.

"Ha! No, I have to go to work."

"And after, is that when you will meet your boyfriend?"

"Actually, I am single—"

"I can see from the look in your eyes that is not exactly a choice, is it, Charity?"

"Well, I have a crush on someone, and tonight I am going to tell him. I'm kinda nervous," she confessed.

"My dear, if he has even one brain cell still functioning in his head, he will scoop you up and run away with you. I know quality when I see it, and you have it, child. Yes, indeed," he said and patted her hand. "You be a good girl now."

"Yes, sir. Thank you, Mr. K. I hope I will get to see you before your stay is over. Merry Christmas," she said, and waved goodbye as she raced to her car.

She did not hear the elderly man whisper his reply softly as he watched her go with sparkling blue eyes, "I'll be watching you, Charity Smith."

He knows if you've been bad or good...

G RAB YOUR COPY OF BEARING GIFTS TODAY.

ABOUT THE AUTHOR

C.D. Gorri is a USA Today Bestselling author of steamy paranormal romance and urban fantasy. She is the creator of the Grazi Kelly Universe.

Join her mailing list here: https://www.cdgorri.com/newsletter

An avid reader with a profound love for books and literature, when she is not writing or taking care of her family, she can usually be found with a book or tablet in hand. C.D. lives in her home state of New Jersey where many of her characters or stories are based. Her tales are fast paced yet detailed with satisfying conclusions.

If you enjoy powerful heroines and loyal heroes who face relatable problems in supernatural settings, journey into the Grazi Kelly Universe today. You will find sassy, curvy heroines and sexy, love-driven heroes who find their HEAs between the pages. Werewolves, Bears, Dragons, Tigers, Witches, Romani, Lynxes, Foxes, Thunderbirds, Vampires, and many more Shifters and supernatural creatures dwell within her worlds. The most important thing is every mate in this universe is fated, loyal, and true lovers always get their happily ever afters.

Want to know how it all began? Enter the Grazi Kelly Universe with Wolf Moon: A Grazi Kelly Novel or pick up Charley's Christmas Wolf and dive into the Macconwood Pack Novel Series today.

For a complete list of C.D. Gorri's books visit her website here:

https://www.cdgorri.com/complete-book-list/

Thank you and happy reading!

del mare alla stella,
    C.D. Gorri

Follow C.D. Gorri here:
    http://www.cdgorri.com
    https://www.facebook.com/Cdgorribooks

https://www.bookbub.com/authors/c-d-gorri
https://twitter.com/cgor22
https://instagram.com/cdgorri/
https://www.goodreads.com/cdgorri
https://www.tiktok.com/@cdgorriauthor

www.ingramcontent.com/pod-product-compliance
Lightning Source LLC
Chambersburg PA
CBHW072028220726
48293CB00016B/576